This Book Is for You If:

You've got a closet full of clothes but feel that you never have anything to wear

Dressing every morning seems a chore

You sometimes shop 'til you drop, but your purchases don't seem to work

You are rarely satisfied with the way you look and what you're wearing

You're tired of not looking your best

HarperSpotlight

How to Find Your Personal Style and Look Fantastic Every Day!

Simple Isn't Easy

by Olivia Goldsmith and Amy Fine Collins

HarperPaperbacks
A Division of HarperCollins*Publishers*

HarperPaperbacks *A Division of* HarperCollins*Publishers*
10 East 53rd Street, New York, N.Y. 10022

Cover and interior art design, direction and illustration by Donald F. Reuter

First printing: September 1995

Printed in the United States of America

HarperPaperbacks, HarperSpotlight, and colophon are trademarks of HarperCollins*Publishers*

❖ 10 9 8 7 6 5 4 3 2

Table
of
Contents

Foreword
Some Notes Before We Begin
xi

1. THE FASHION TRAP
or Why Most Women Don't Look Good
*Defining the problem of achieving
personal style*
1

2. FEAR AND CLOTHING
or Pitiful Pitfalls
*The sixteen fears that stand between you
and true style*
17

3. SIMPLE ISN'T EASY
or The Zen Approach to Style
*How to clean out your closet, develop your own style,
make some money doing it and find the real you*
29

4. SELF-ASSESSMENT
or Mirror, Mirror on the Wall
*How to discover what you really look like—and what
you can achieve with that*
47

5. COMFORT vs. STYLE
or The Balancing Act
Resolving the tension between looking *good and* feeling *good*
65

6. WEIGHT A MINUTE!
or A Waist Is a Terrible Thing to Mind
Why your weight is no excuse for not looking good
right now
73

7. STRATEGIES
or Six Never-Fail Fixes
Six simple solutions to dressing with simplicity, style
and flair
81

8. GETTING HELP
or Finding a Fashion Guru
How to get effective help
91

9. DRESS REHEARSAL
or I Thought I Liked It When I Put It On
Trying out your new wardrobe and refining it
103

10. SHOPPING
or A Dangerous Game
How to shop and still keep that closet lean
115

11. ACCESSORIES AFTER THE FACT
or Finishing Touches
How to choose the accessories you need and eliminate those you don't
131

12. MAINTAINING THE LEAN CLOSET
or Keeping It Down
How to make your closet your ally, not your enemy
151

13. GROOMING AND MAINTENANCE
or Care and Breeding
Tender loving care of your clothes, skin, hair, nails, etc.
163

14. CHANGING YOUR STYLE
or What? After All This Work!
When to upgrade or alter your personal style
189

In Closing
201

Letter to Readers
202

FOREWORD

Some Notes Before We Begin

"Beauty of style and harmony and grace and good rhythm depend on simplicity."

—Plato

This book began when I spent a year researching the fashion industry for my third novel, *Fashionably Late*. I spent a lot of time reading about or talking to American designers, staff, magazine editors, fashion writers, models, fashion photographers, and others who create the clothes and the images that affect all of us. But far more interesting to me were the interviews with "civilians"—normal women whom I met in the malls and department stores all across the country. Some women loved to shop. Others hated it. Some had unlimited budgets; others had to shop the sales and pinch pennies. But one thing I found consistently: no matter whom I spoke to, one irony stood out sharply. ***There wasn't one woman who felt that she had the right clothes.*** And I also found that shopping, the actual act of looking and purchasing, had become the American woman's personal obsession. I felt it was important to examine why so many women were obsessed with clothing and shopping. And I also had to examine the way the "garmentos"—the uncreative, money-grubbing element of the fashion industry—often feed that obsession or, even worse, take advantage of it.

So I finished the novel, but I also began to examine the way *I* myself dressed, shopped and felt about clothes. The answers were complex and confusing, so I continued my research. Now, after an exhaustive eight-month process, I have reached a kind of personal fashion enlightenment. Like all enlightenment, it is simple—but not easy. It didn't happen overnight and it wasn't exactly what I expected, but if you feel that you could and should look better-dressed than you do, this *Simple Isn't Easy* approach to style may be the answer.

The second irony I discovered in my research was the key to it all: that those most knowledgeable in the fashion world didn't buy into all the trends and fads of fashion. It was their version of the doctor's "clinical detachment"—to dress in a "uniform" that did not distract them. Most of them had developed a style of their own, and stuck with it. It seemed to free them from insecurity and the kind of fashion slavery the rest of us were victims of, while at the same time it defined them more effectively than the lush fashion photographs they helped to design and publish. I was lucky enough to interview some of the most knowledgeable people on New York's Seventh Avenue, the center of American garment design. And I began to see that there was a need, not just for my novel but for a book that would help today's women find a way out of the maze that fashion has become.

I promise that by following a few simple (but not necessarily easy) steps you can:

- **Look better-dressed each and every day**
- **Spend less time on dressing and shopping**
- **Spend less money on clothes**
- **Have better-organized clothes and roomier closets**
- **Make some money in the process**
- **Help less fortunate people**.

No, I'm not suggesting joining a Carmelite convent (although the monastic look *was* big a couple of seasons ago). Nor that you forget about style and wear jeans and sweats the rest of your life. It's my own belief that the female of our species, from earliest times, has had an instinctive, sensuous delight in ornamentation. (I'm sure there were cave women who wouldn't be caught dead in a fig leaf—they felt they were more the bamboo type.) And I look on that as a uniquely female, healthy and creative form of self-expression. But it is an impulse that has undone us, as I'll show you.

I also believe that style must come not from without, but within. As D. T. Suzuki wrote, about Zen—but it applies equally to style—"Zen in its essence is the art of seeing into the nature of one's being, and it points the way from bondage to freedom." Each of us can find our own freedom and take back the pleasure that is our birthright. Style enlightenment—like the more profound Zen kind—can be obtained through meditation and self-contemplation, rather than from a TV commercial, magazine layout or some other ultimately disappointing external source.

But I am smart enough to know what I *don't* know. Not only do I know that I can't (and won't) tell other women how to dress, I also knew I wasn't expert enough in the higher issues of aesthetics and style to undertake a project like this by myself. So I asked Amy Fine Collins, style editor of *Harper's Bazaar* and contributing editor at *Vanity Fair*, to help me. Universally admired, her art and fashion history background, her unrivalled sense of style and her practical working knowledge of the fashion industry have helped to make this book what it is. So, though I use my voice throughout, Amy has written as much of the book as I have and edited every word.

Throughout the book we've quoted experts and designers we admire. Not because we think you must buy their clothes, but because these artists have studied the problem of self-presentation and have practical advice we can all apply.

Our purpose is to simplify issues for you about who you are and how you want to look. I know that simple isn't easy. Still, it seems to me that women in the Nineties—with both greater self-awareness and a greater ecological concern than ever before—are ready to step off the trend treadmill and, instead, acquire real and lasting personal style. We are not giving directions in this book, but rather pointing out much which you already know. We are not telling you what to wear, but rather giving you the tools to help you decide. We hope we are directing you to a path you have been seeking for some time. If this book helps you to do that, I'm glad.

Olivia Goldsmith

Ever since I was able to buckle my own Mary Janes, and probably even before then, I have loved clothing. My favorite toys were Barbie, the ultimate fashion plate, and paper dolls, whose outfits I often drew myself. I remember with perfect clarity all of my mother's wardrobe from my childhood. (She had gone to Paris to study fashion, but wound up an art historian instead.) And to this day I recall events by recollecting what I wore on a particular occasion. Always I adored the beauty, magic and fantasy of fashion magazines, never imagining that I would one day work for one. My southern childhood encouraged a fondness for feminine fripperies, but never at the expense of my other interests.

It makes me sad that something that has been a great source of pleasure to me can cause confusion, unhappiness and anxiety in other women. Women are often misled into supposing that they should resemble the images in fashion magazines. This is a misunderstanding of their purpose. They are meant for inspiration, fantasy and admiration, not for imitation. Every historical era needs its ideals of beauty. The ancient Greeks had their sculptures of Venus, the Renaissance its icons of the Madonna. But as these cultures were not consumer societies, they regarded these feminine images as sensual or spiritual paragons—visions to contemplate, not emulate. All civilized societies need to generate images of beauty, and these should be pleasurable, not threatening, to behold. One aim of this book is to help you to distinguish between the public ideal of beauty and your own personal standard, and to dress and groom yourself accordingly.

Adorning oneself to enhance one's attractiveness is a very basic, powerful urge. I hope that instead of denying, thwarting, or abusing this instinct you can cultivate and master it.

If you feel overwhelmed by too many choices, too many images, and confused by conflicting needs to be an individual yet conform to a peer group, you are not alone. Even the designers and fashion editors who make and present the clothes you see in shops and magazines are baffled about why, given all the merchandise out there and all the direction given by magazines, American women still have such trouble establishing a good-looking wardrobe.

Fashion has become so pluralistic and changes occur so quickly that it is not surprising that women have lost their bearings. Short and long hemlines, square-toed and pointy shoes, dramatic and understated makeup can all chicly coexist in one single season. It was easier to be stylish when only one look at a time reigned supreme. But when fashion dictates, along with so many other social institutions, were deemed obsolete in the Sixties, they were overthrown.

Happily, we are not headed back to a time of universal conformity. So as long as fashion remains a large and varied garden from which you may pluck what you please, you might as well have a guidebook to lead you to what is best and most becoming for you. *Simple Isn't Easy* will help steer you away from disorder, disillusionment and disaster and toward a simpler, clearer, more stylish path.

After all, we do want to look our best. Our appearance should be a source of pride and pleasure to ourselves, and those around us. Feeling good about the way you look frees you to go about the business of your life with more confidence and satisfaction.

There is an art to being stylish, but not all of us are artists. A natural gift for fashion is as rare as a special talent for painting. Interestingly, many fashion professionals, myself included, are would-be artists who have transferred their creative energies from one field to the other. Expertise in both fashion and art requires a feeling for proportion, scale, composition, and color—a combination of heightened visual awareness, fearlessness, and rigorous self-scrutiny. Yet few women expect to be accomplished painters (otherwise how-to-draw books would be topping the best-seller lists). Why, then, do so many of us strive to be accomplished dressers?

Well, one good reason is that every one of us wears clothes. And don't you agree that, since getting dressed is an act that we all must perform at least once a day, better to go about it with enjoyment and self-awareness than with blindness and timidity? Achieving a sense of style is not only a wonderful gift to yourself, it is a generous gesture to all those who see you. We don't want to be like the child who thinks no one notices her just because she has shut her eyes. What's on your body communicates to the world what's on your mind.

I hope *Simple Isn't Easy* helps you to think more clearly about who you are and how you look. Whether your taste is conservative or flamboyant, your wardrobe is your most public and direct form of self-expression. The great news is that beauty, youth or sex appeal are not necessary to achieve style. In fact, they can be a hindrance. And of all these traits, style alone endures. This is something to celebrate.

Amy Fine Collins

THE FASHION TRAP

or

Why Most Women Don't Look Good

> "Fashion is made
> to go out of fashion."
> —Coco Chanel

Is getting dressed each morning a problem? Do you hate what you see in your closet or, worse yet, in your mirror? How come?

Well, you're not alone. Do you know that in Europe American women tourists are mocked for their lack of style? "Why are all American women so badly dressed?" one Italian journalist asked me. "They are not poor, or stupid, but they wear jogging suits out to dinner." (To be fair, one should remember that in *her* country even the *men* spend 25 percent of their income on clothing.) "And why are American women so fat and always eating in public? And why are they squeezed into their clothes?" asked a French friend. "Nothing fits. And they are always underdressed or overdressed." Well, *you* know about the French! They believe they're superior and they don't mind telling you! But what gives?

I don't know about you, but these questions made *me* take several steps backwards! Were they talking about me? Was I, too, fashion impaired? What a painful realization to accept! If you're in doubt about your own sense of style (and you must be or you wouldn't have bought this book) try this tongue-in-chic quiz.

Learn If You're Fashion Impaired, Savvy or Middle Ground

Do you tell people that fashion doesn't interest you, but secretly envy your friend with the beautiful wardrobe? **Y N**

Have you ever left the house with mismatched shoes on your feet? **Y N**

Are you ignored by sales clerks when you go to shop? **Y N**

Did you seriously consider re-wearing the bridesmaid dress from your high school best friend's wedding? **Y N**

Do occasions that require you to dress up make you shudder? **Y N**

Do you live in jogging suits even though you haven't been near a gym in months? **Y N**

Do you forget the last time you received a compliment for how you looked? (Was it in this decade?) **Y N**

Have you already forgotten what you were wearing yesterday? **Y N**

Do you consider *Field & Stream* a fashion magazine? **Y N**

How to score the quiz

All no's = Good for you! Return this book! You *already* have all the fashion savvy you need.
1–3 no's = Middle ground: This book can help.
4–9 no's = Bad news: You are one of the fashion-impaired. You really need this book!

Well, how fashion savvy are you? Where do you fall on the spectrum between Fashion-Impaired and Super-Stylish? Or do you fall off the chart completely?

It was a painful realization, to admit that European women had a valid point: most American women *don't* look well dressed. And this doesn't mean that we aren't wearing fashionable clothes, or that we aren't trying. Actually, some women were trying *too* hard and their desperation showed. (But at least you have to give them special credit for effort.)

In search of answers, I began to carefully observe American women. I saw women wearing beautiful clothes that fit poorly, women wearing colors that complemented their shoes but not their skin tone. I saw women who seemed to have given up: I saw women whose outfits proclaimed: "More gold!" or, "More fabrics! More ruffles! More sequins!" They looked like dinner plates piled with ice cream, potato chips *and* chocolate syrup—all flavor and no nourishment—which is to say "No Taste."

What, then, causes the problem? How had all of this come to pass? As I continued my research, three reasons for the problem became clear:

- **Too much stuff**

- **The influence of evil "garmentos"**

- **The lack of concentration**

Too Much Stuff

One of the answers is that American women actually take dressing too much for granted and that, my dear, is part of the problem. For the first time in history, clothes are readily available off the rack. They are reduced to an impulse buy. This leads to too much stuff.

In the past, right up to the early part of this century, clothes were made by the wearer or by seamstresses to order. This meant that women thought long and hard before they cut into that bolt of merino wool. They wore a mistake for years. In the Eighteenth century, the emerging middle-class woman might have had only three or four dresses, adding one as another wore out.

Now, too often, we try to solve wardrobe problems by throwing money at them. And, like most problems, money is not the solution. More stuff actually makes *more* style problems, not fewer.

The Influence of Evil "Garmentos"

We have all had the experience of closets stuffed with clothes, coupled with the feeling we have nothing to wear. How does it happen? It is not *only* the availability of ready-to-wear garments, or our lack of self-control.

For years I had heard the misguided theory that designers—usually, according to this theory, male and gay—hated women and came up with ridiculous designs to make us all look bad. (I even planned a character like that for my novel.) But what I found, in reality, was that designers—male and female, whatever their sexual orientation—seemed to *like* women and their vision was most often of a beautiful, fluid bonding of a woman with her clothes. Their designs may not always work, and some are certainly guilty of designing only for the ideal woman's body (or an adolescent boy's!), but there is no hatred or conspiracy.

If there *is* a conspiracy, it does not come from the creative people in fashion. The designers, stylists, photographers, editors and reporters that I met were all—to a greater or lesser degree—sincerely entranced with fashion. And they are most often stylish people that one could learn from, and who are usually happy to teach. But there is both cynicism and condescension toward women on the part of the businessmen who run the financial side of the industry. These guys—I call them "garmentos"—spend their business lives hyping whatever products they are selling this season, getting them produced as cheaply as possible and pushing them into the stores. They exploit labor and their customers. Evil garmentos are not the rule, but they do exist, living and thriving in both the manufacturing and the retail side of the business. And we are their victims.

Now, I suppose they are no worse than businessmen in the tobacco industry: They have us hooked and they mean to make it pay. But they do so by advertising in a way that makes us feel inferior and fearful, if we don't get in line. They sell *fashion* instead of *style*. And you better know the difference, girlfriend! As Yves Saint Laurent put it, "Fashion changes but style is eternal." If you get trapped into buying this season's latest do-dah even though it doesn't suit you and you feel awful in it, it is only partly your fault. The evil garmentos have struck another victim down. We're going to tell you how to stop letting that happen. And how to save a lot of money.

Lack of Concentration

Money aside for the moment, how much *thought* and *effort* do you want to put into your personal style?

For some women like my friend Greta, a single mother and investment banker, the answer is "not a lot." She's a no-nonsense, practical type. But the Gretas of the world still have a slightly nagging feeling that they could look better than they currently do. For Vivian, a film student, almost *any* level of effort seems worth the reward of feeling and looking attractive and comfortable. If you fall into either category or, as is most likely, somewhere in the middle, the *Simple Isn't Easy* method will work for you. But remember that fashion and style are only as important as *you* want them to be.

It's my impression that women care a lot. But that does not mean that we know what to do about it. Why? Now, there *are* those social psychologists who would say that Americans are still burdened with a Puritan fear that looking stylish or being vain about your appearance is somehow a sin. I'm not sure about that, but what I *am* sure about is the reluctance we have to focus deeply on how we want to look—considering what is possible and what is not. Perhaps it is only a question of time, or the lack of it, which prevents some of us from really scrutinizing our looks and our style. Perhaps it is simply easier to be blinded to our faults and limitations than to cope with them. Maybe it's an inability to see, or to diagnose. And perhaps it is impossible not to be swayed by the evil garmentos. For whatever the reason, despite money spent, most women don't actually successfully focus on how they want to look or, if they do, they fail to come up with a plan to achieve that look.

I admit it isn't easy. In the past, even the recent past, women didn't work and spent more time at home in comfortable, not-for-public wear, like the housedress (remember them?). They "got dressed" to be seen publicly and that meant they had both the blueprint on how they were expected to look and the time to take great care: even a generation ago, some women were taught to wear hats and gloves in public places. But with the evolution of the working woman, *we got used to being seen in public and stopped preparing.* After all, we have so much else to do now. That is the heart of the problem. *Because getting dressed in an attractive, appropriate and comfortable way is a difficult task.*

I talked all of these insights over with Amy. She added the missing piece. In addition to too much stuff, evil garmentos and the lack of concentration, she was surprised that many women didn't follow the three unwritten principles of taste. Unwritten principles? *What unwritten principles?* Was this some secret code that I, too, had been unaware of?

Actually, they are the building blocks this book is based on. That, and the practical hints I needed to achieve them. They are appropriateness, understatement and ease.

Unwritten Principle of Taste No. 1: Appropriateness

Some women I saw at one particular Florida mall wore hooker-wear that had no sexual subtlety, while others wore corporate armor plates that had no subtle sexuality. While hooker-looks may work on the fashion runway or at a sophisticated nightclub and asexuality is *de rigueur* on business women at board meetings, there in the mall "shocking" looked pathetic and "stuffy" merely looked like taxidermy. As Eleanor Lambert, creator of the Best Dressed List, told us, "Wearing too little in public is what I detest most for a woman."

Appropriateness means more than dressing for the place and the occasion. It also means projecting a positive and accurate awareness of who you are. Some women with lively, interesting, kind and loving demeanors were dressed so drably that they seemed to disappear into a marshmallow blob of rosebeige poly, sandblasted denim and foam soles, while others wore outfits so coordinated, so busy or so bold that they, too, vanished—whatever was special about their faces, personalities or presences drowned out by their outfits' roar.

The late Grace Kelly, Princess of Appropriateness (and Monaco), knew that in the U.S. appropriateness means blending in, whereas in European society it means sticking out a bit. So for everyday wear, as a debutante and then as an ingenue actress, she favored cashmere twinsets, white gloves, pearls and clean-scrubbed skin and hair. But once she was a princess, for social events or official occasions she donned a diamond tiara, upswept hair and discreetly glamorous gowns.

Unwritten Principle of Taste No. 2:
Understatement

The concept here is that you've got a statement to make and it's so worthwhile, it can speak gently; you don't need to knock everybody's eyes out to get it across. Understatement generally means choosing clean lines over choppy, fussy, elaborate silhouettes, using a few harmonious colors to good effect, and showing small splashes of brightness, dazzle, bare skin, etc. rather than oceans of anything. Note that understatement does NOT mean self-effacement: "I want to vanish so that no one notices how flawed I am," translates into "Nobody has flaws but me," which is both unattractively self-pitying and grossly unobservant. Think of Cindy Crawford's mole. She kept it. She uses it to proclaim that she's unique. But you'll notice that she doesn't make a big deal of it by painting zillions of beauty marks all over. Designer Carolina Herrera has made polka dots her trademark—she even uses them on her perfume packages—but she uses them sparingly. You would never see this classic, serene beauty clownishy dressed in an overwhelming head-to-toe polka-dot statement.

Unwritten Principle of Taste No. 3:
Ease and Grace

How do we define it? The appearance of being comfortable and confident, not only in your understated, appropriate outfit, but in Capital-L "Life." As Bill Blass puts it succinctly, "Self-confidence is what gives a woman style." Early in her husband's presidency, Nancy Reagan wore her fastidious assemblages of matching buttons, jewels and shoes with as much aplomb as anyone could, but the obsessive coordination of it all was exhausting to behold, what we call "too matchey-matchey." You expected her to come into your house and start flicking soot flecks off of the sills. You could always tell that being judged by the public was torture for her.

Isabella Rossellini, the actress and model, on the other hand, always looks relaxed, whether she's in a bathing suit or an evening gown. It's not just because she's beautiful either; it's because she comfortably wears clothes that announce (quietly) that she feels good about how she looks. As one designer put it, "an appearance of naturalness is essential to style."

Why is it that so few of us have absorbed these principles, even if we have learned so many other of life's lessons? Part of the reason, I think, is that each of us is expected to reinvent the wheel. If you want to learn music, there are methods; you start with scales, master an instrument, and gradually increase your knowledge and ability until you can work your own variations on what has come before. But if you want to learn to dress with style, you're expected to invent yourself from whole cloth all on your own. And, ironically, you are overwhelmed with choices and conflicting advice in newspapers, magazines and on TV. So most women end up improvising variations on fashion's themes before they learn fashion's basics. Anyone can develop style, but if you're not, like Amy, born with it, and your job isn't in the performing or fine arts, the place to start is by evolving your personal version of good taste before attempting revisions of it. This doesn't mean dressing just like Grace, Jackie, Cindy, Carolina or Isabella but it usually means mastering the principles that they embody: Quality, balance, awareness of self and place, subtlety, ease. As Mary McFadden told us, "The thing that gives a woman style is an imaginative mind that creates elegance."

The Uniform

How to put this all into practice? The most fascinating thing I observed was that all of the stylish people in the fashion business had stopped following fashion! What they had instead was what I call "a uniform." Though it varied widely from person to person, each of them had selected what worked best for them and then seemed to stick with it. This gave them not only ease in dressing, but also a visible identity. This book aims to help you do the same. It means you must give up promiscuous shopping, fad-following and self-hatred. It means you must take a clear and accurate look at yourself and the way you live. It means you must clean out your closet and admit your mistakes.

But what you'll get in return is a clear sense of your own uniform and a simplicity in both getting dressed and in your looks. With luck this will develop even further into your own personal style.

We have chosen not to make *Simple Isn't Easy* a book of Dos and Don'ts because we both hate the idea of commandments (Amy's first instinct is to bend, twist, break and challenge rules)—and because we want to encourage you to find *your own, personal* style. Yet, as you may have noticed, at the same time we don't endorse an "anything goes" outlook on getting dressed. We do have opinions, and strong ones, on what constitutes personal style. *We are, for example, against any individual looks that are self-destructive, self-denying, or that arise out of fear or ignorance.* The "I-don't-know-anything-about-style-but-I-know-what-I-like" attitude does not work for us either. If you make judgments and choices about clothing, you should know *why* you make them. If you know not just what you like but *why* you like it, then you have learned something not only about fashion but also about style—and yourself. Finally, remember here that we are talking about clothes, but not only about clothes. In the words of Valentino, "Quality in fashion is determined by workmanship, beautiful fabrics, the finishing and details. But often, all this does not add quality to a woman herself. For a woman quality is something within her."

Q&A

Designer

Q: What is the most common wardrobe mistake you see women commit?

A: The total matching look. The labels too "visible."

—*Christian Louboutin*

FEAR AND CLOTHING

or

Pitiful Pitfalls

> "Were the diver to think on the jaws of the shark he would never lay hands on the precious pearl."
> —SA'DI

Now that we've separated the good guys from the bad guys and handed you some guiding principles, we'd also like to acquaint you with some common pitfalls that may undermine *your* best efforts at style. We've identified a number of bad, unacceptable reasons that women may have for dressing as they do—and the kinds of looks that arise from them. And, in this chapter we're going to define them. If you recognize your mode in one of these categories, it will be the first step toward finding your way out, and into a stylishness all your own. Now, we're *not* going to give you news about what height heels are in or out. Instead, what each of these categories has in common—and why you should steer clear of them—is that they all arise from *FEAR*, a crippling and blinding emotion.

Personal style invariably arises from security. Do you, instead of dressing in what pleases you, succumb to these fears? Are you:

Afraid of Looking Too Rich?

Sometimes called "reverse chic" or "reverse snobbism," this look is popular among old money or guilty liberals and/or feminists. You know the look: pilled polyester dresses instead of lovely silk; out-of-date, frayed frumpiness that does not make the wearer look better (or fool anyone about her solvency). "Dressing down" is really just a way of putting yourself down.

?   **Afraid of Looking Too Poor?**

This fear usually results in piling on glittering junk—gilt buttons, knock-offs of more expensive garments, scarves and shoes. The result is almost always the reverse of the intended effect. Trying desperately to imitate an expensive style you can't afford only makes your attempt look cheap compared to the real thing. Try, instead, for something genuine *and* within your means.

?   **Afraid of Looking Too Conformist?**

You've seen this: It results in a detestable fake rebel effect: body piercing, tattoos, too much leather, unwashed jeans, all imitating an authentic rebel style from the past (hippie, beatnik, punk). Ironically, "rebel without a cause" looks are often the most conformist looks around. (Adolescents often put themselves in this trap, but they're excused. They can plead raging hormones and the painful slide into adulthood.) If you simply like tattoos, terrific. But if you think you're being avant garde, ask yourself this: How can you be a nonconformist when thousands of others are also sporting holey blue jeans, nose rings, and shaved heads? Silly you.

? Afraid of Looking Too Out of the Ordinary?

Ah, the deadly corporate clone or suburban Stepford Wife effect! We know that many professions, offices, and even neighborhoods have an unwritten dress code, and remember we're all for appropriateness, but we challenge you to be as creative and individual as possible within that code. If you look at a group of uniformed schoolgirls you will notice dozens of incredibly imaginative but subtly individual touches that make some uniforms more personal—variations in skirt length, sock folding, collar shape, or just the manner of rolling up sleeves. Apply this same principle to your own peer group's appropriate gear.

? Afraid of Looking Too Sexy?

I'm a victim of this fear, which all too often results in loose, shapeless, buttoned-up, uptight or mannish clothes. In the corporate world I hoped it would fend off harassment. (It didn't.) In my private life, I thought it would camouflage my weight and make me more appealing. Boy, was that wrong! With this kind of fear, a woman looks stiff or unsensual, unapproachable and undesirable—not just to men, but to other women, children and pets. (Well, actually, my beagle still loved me.)

Susan Jedren, a New York novelist and good friend, pointed this pitfall out to me. Susan wears formfitting turtleneck sweaters and cinched-waisted slacks. "I feel comfortable looking hot. We should be free to express ourselves this way. It's fun." And it definitely is Susan.

? **Afraid of Not Looking Sexy Enough?**

You know what this results in. Don't you feel sorry for the would-be vamps out there who usually model themselves after some soap or rock star or other unrealistic role model? Too much hair, noisy jewelry, cheap perfume, ill-fitting, tight clothes. If that describes you, get a grip! Men will know you're a woman without the rubber skirt and the tube top. Pierre Cardin, the great French designer, knows all about this fear. "It's stupid if you need to see everything that a woman is," he said. "You must use your imagination. If you see immediately, the charm is finished, you know. It's like a book. If you know everything immediately, it is not exciting." Sexiness is about mystery, not about being obvious.

? **Afraid of Standing Out?**

Also known as the "who, me?" or wallflower effect, this fear usually results in slovenliness, bad posture, and faded, dreary colors that blend into skin tones. If, when you sit on a beige sofa in a waiting room, you become invisible, you're a victim of this fear. Elegance can be quiet, but it must also be *confident*.

As Emanuel Ungaro puts it, "A woman who correctly interprets one's look never becomes a fashion victim. Being a real woman, confident, active and modern are the right ingredients of true elegance."

? Afraid of Blending In?

The opposite of the above-mentioned "who, me?" syndrome, this fear results in attention-getting but unflattering hats, general loudness in color of clothes and makeup, clanging jewelry, lots of rhinestones, noisy high heels and flashing gimcracks on shoes, belts and even sweatshirts. For victims of this problem, remember this: Sometimes the best way to be heard is to whisper.

? Afraid of Looking Too Old?

Well, in this youth-obsessed society, aren't we all? But when that fear results in dressing like a teenager when you're middle-aged, you've got a problem. (In our opinion, sometimes even *teenagers* should not dress like teenagers!) Dressing much younger than your years only makes you look older by contrast— just like lying about your age does. This fear can also have you jumping on trends without really pausing to consider whether they are flattering or appropriate. Who wants to look like mutton dressed as lamb? And who do you fool? Youthfulness is a question of attitude and energy, not young clothing.

Afraid of Looking Too Young?

Most of us outgrow this by our late twenties but, whenever it occurs, it results in a forced sophistication that looks awkward and disguises the true appeal of youth. Common mistakes from this fear include too much "good" jewelry, fur coats, very high heels, too much makeup—a kind of jailbait effect. Learn from your elders, but don't dress like them—yet. There's plenty of time for that. As the French say, "Elegance is the privilege of age."

Afraid of Looking Too Casual?

Hey, Little Miss Perfect, loosen up! (Even if your "loosening up" is as carefully calculated as your every outfit.) Unbutton a button, push up your sweater sleeves, slacken the knot tying your scarf. Good clothes are designed to move, to be fluid. Otherwise you look like a prim, flawlessly wrapped gift package with nothing inside.

Afraid of Looking Too Formal?

God, those women in bicycle pants and sneakers at the museum, in ski jackets at the theater! Show a little respect for the hostess of your party, the city you're visiting, for the old friends you're meeting for dinner—

and for yourself. Sloppy, dirty, messy—the "I just got back from an Outward Bound week and haven't had time to change" look—just doesn't work except in the wilderness.

?   Afraid of Seeming Too Stylish?

Yes, there can be a fearful overreaction to the latest issue of *Allure*. (This is not a new problem. One of Edith Wharton's characters in *The Age of Innocence* was so afraid of appearing too fashionable she used to store her Paris purchases in a box for a year before she wore them!) If *you* become terrified and overwhelmed by the new, it may mean you'll never change your style—even when you've outgrown it. You'll be lost in a time warp with your too-short coat and too-long dress. This fear produces women who seem to derive no pleasure from clothing, or for that matter from life. Consider the words of Joubert: "There may be less vanity in following the new modes than in adhering to the old ones."

?   Afraid of Seeming Too Unstylish?

The reverse of the above, it results in slavish fashion faddism as a substitute for style—piling on everything you saw in an advertisement or a runway shot.

It makes you look like you have no judgment of your own. And it costs piles of money to keep on the fashion treadmill. Interestingly, many of the top fashion designers we polled told us, as Bill Blass did, that "following fashion diminishes a woman's style the most."

?   Afraid You're Trying Too Hard?

If you look like you don't care, then you seem as if you don't care about yourself either. And so why should anyone care about you? Take pride in your appearance. There's no shame in it, no matter what you've been told. Put on some makeup, press your clothes, try on a pair of comfortable heels.

?   Afraid You're Not Trying Hard Enough?

If you try too hard then your anxiety and tension show. Too much concern about matching colors, patterns and textures looks fussy, overwrought and frightened. Relax, loosen up, eliminate, be sparing. Dress for who you are, not whom you want others to mistake you for. Giorgio Armani, my Zeus in the Pantheon of designer gods, told me, "Do not force yourself to look like something you're not. Naturalness is synonymous with style."

So, go through this mini-quiz and check the boxes appropriate for you. Are you afraid of

Looking too rich	☐ ☐	Looking too poor
Looking too conformist	☐ ☐	Looking too out of the ordinary
Looking too sexy	☐ ☐	Not looking sexy enough
Standing out too much	☐ ☐	Blending in too much
Looking too old	☐ ☐	Looking too young
Looking too casual	☐ ☐	Looking too formal
Seeming too stylish	☐ ☐	Seeming too unstylish
Trying too hard	☐ ☐	Not trying hard enough

How many fears do you have? Finally, ask yourself, "Who is the audience I'm trying to please?" The only valid answer, as far as we're concerned, is YOURSELF. Here two designers concentrated our views concisely: Fernando Sanchez's basic advice on style was "Be yourself—work with what you feel," while Todd Oldham said, "Dress for yourself only."

But you must recognize your own fears and overcome them yourself. If you are a victim of any of these fears, we can help you eliminate them. What we are proposing in the rest of this book is a way to feel and look better with less effort, but it requires self-examination and mindfulness. Only you can do it for yourself. In the rest of *Simple Isn't Easy* we suggest the following: a combination of meditations and actions to achieve a more stylish and simplified wardrobe. Here are the steps.

Cleaning out your closet and finding the real you (Chapter 3)

Discovering what you really look like—and what you can achieve with that (Chapter 4)

Resolving the tension between *looking* good and *feeling* good (Chapter 5)

Why your weight is no excuse for not looking good *right now* (Chapter 6)

Six solutions to dressing with simplicity, style and flair (Chapter 7)

Finding a fashion guru (Chapter 8)

Trying out your new wardrobe and refining it (Chapter 9)

Shopping and still keeping that closet lean (Chapter 10)

Choosing the accessories you need and eliminating those you don't (Chapter 11)

Making your closet your ally, not your enemy (Chapter 12)

Taking loving care of your clothes, skin, hair, nails, etc. (Chapter 13)

Knowing when to upgrade or alter your personal style (Chapter 14)

SIMPLE ISN'T EASY

EASY

or

The Zen Approach to Style

> "It's better to lose than acquire."
> —Boris Pasternak

It wasn't easy getting dressed each morning. I mean, I didn't know where to start. I'd pick a blouse or maybe a skirt I felt like wearing and then something to go with it, but the top didn't look right without a belt, and I didn't have a belt in the right color that was thin enough for the skirt, and it was already past eight-fifteen. You know, I always figured my problems getting dressed were a combination of poor planning and not enough stuff. I believed that if I just got the *right* thin belt, then I'd be okay. Right? Wrong!

Of course, like everyone else who's ever been to Paris, I'd noticed the way French women put themselves together. It always impressed me—so chic, but so simple—especially considering the cost of good clothes there. I asked a secretary (I knew how little she was paid) how she did it. And she told me: "I only buy one new outfit a season. First, I window-shop a lot, to see what would suit me. Then I focus on a few things. I try them on several times. Then sometimes I even wait until I can buy one on sale. I certainly wait until I know that it suits me and I love it."

"I certainly wait until I know that it suits me and I love it." Well, it's not the American way, but I was willing to admit that after more than twenty years of buying my own clothes, I didn't look the way I wanted to. And the solution (though I tried it every season) simply couldn't be more clothes, or different clothes. Perhaps it was *fewer* clothes. How Nineties! How ecological!

30

In fact, the size and number of closets in American homes puzzle European visitors. And, typically American, our most natural reaction to fashion confusion is to go out and buy more stuff. Well, that doesn't work. As shoe designer Manolo Blahnik observed: "It is a question of selection, to choose less. That is something Americans do not understand. They think that more is better." Like most problems, it can't be solved simply by throwing money at it.

Simple Isn't Easy outlines a way for you to decide on your own best look, to create a wardrobe based on that and to come up with an almost foolproof way of dressing in a lot less time with much better results than you have today. By now you should know this book does not recommend—in fact, it condemns—the idea that the answer to your personal style lies in something external. You don't need just one more blazer, another pair of shoes or the right purse. And you certainly don't need one of those stupid, facile "how-to-dress-like-a-man-for-success" recipes, or a magazine article's list of this year's must haves: one pleated skirt, one navy blazer, etc, etc.

Because, despite spending incredible amounts of time and throwing lots of money at the problem, dressing well isn't easy. If it were, ninety out of a hundred women would look good. We have to overcome our fears, see ourselves clearly as what we are and not be deflected from the task by the evil garmentos. Certainly, all of *my* shopping had not yielded me a look I was happy with. And my research for *Fashionably Late* only made me more certain that shopping wasn't the answer. As I was finishing the novel, I happened to read an interview with Andrée Putman, the famous French architect and a veritable *doyenne* of style. "American closets shock me," she said. "So much, too much. No one can dress well with so many clothes." *No one can dress well with so many clothes.*

Well, there it was. The reason, perhaps, why I so rarely felt "right." It couldn't be my taste, could it? I mean, I *know* what I like. I even think I know, usually, what looks good on me. And I know I have nice clothes. So, what's the problem? In a word (okay, make that two), the problem was *too much*.

Well, Amy helped me to discover the principles of style, and even how they might be broken. And she led me away from some fear-induced pitfalls. Though she left me with some clear, gorgeous visions in my head, I still had a murky mess in my closet. Because, my friend, I had shopped. And, like most of us, I had shopped too often and badly.

Let me tell the truth: I had more than enough. My closet proved it! There was the time I was in London in August. Harrods, Harvey Nichols, Nicole Farhi, Joseph Tricot, Charles Jourdan, *all* of them had their final summer markdowns. Irresistible silk olive slacks for only thirty dollars. A navy handknit sweater (I collect them) from Whistles, immorally expensive at three hundred and fifty dollars, but reduced to a hundred and ten. A nifty Ghost T-shirt for forty bucks (if my pound to dollar math was correct.) And that's not counting previous binges (usually at sale time) in Miami's Bal Harbour and all the stuff from The Gap and catalogues.

Reader, it happened again and again. But in London I fell for them all once more. *And* schlepped them back to the hotel. So there I was, lying on my tiny hotel room bed (what is it with those English single beds?) exhausted, having lost the battle of the bulge—none of my suitcases would close. And, once back in New York, none of the closet doors—and I have four, including two walk-ins—would shut.

So my research, my shopping and my closets all conspired to make me face the confusion I had wrought. With Amy's enlightenment guiding me like a golden beacon (and the voice of Andrée Putman ringing in my ears), I came to some important truths about what I feel best dressed in. So I decided, once and for all, that I had more than enough. **That I would do my shopping in my closet, and find out something about myself there**. And that meant a task almost more daunting than cleaning out the Augeon stables. I lead the way, but you can do it too. Here, in seven simple (but not easy) steps you too can achieve simplicity and style.

1. TRY ON EVERYTHING YOU OWN
2. DECIDE ON A LOOK
3. CONTEMPLATE THE TRAGEDIES
4. FURTHER SORT THE GARMENTS
   FROM YOUR "KEEP" PILE
5. SURVEY WHAT YOU HAVE WROUGHT

6. LEARN THE ZEN PHILOSOPHY OF FASHION
7. PRACTICE WEARING THIS STUFF
   FOR A MONTH

STEP ONE: TRY ON EVERYTHING YOU OWN

The first step is, as always, the most important. And the hardest. Most women—those of us who are not gifted with natural chic like Amy—spend a lifetime trying to evolve a look and never really succeed. *But now you will.* It may not, in the end, be your only look, or perhaps even your ultimate look. But you will pick one and stick with it for a while.

The way I decided was by trying on just about everything I had. God, how exhausting. But do it. This is the key to everything. What an exercise! (If you need any more motivation to simplify, this should do the trick.) I put a whole morning aside and I wasn't done by lunch (and I get up *very* early!). So, as you move through the nightmare of your closet, MAKE TWO PILES—THE GOOD AND THE BAD. Looks I liked, I put in one pile; those I didn't, I put in another. (Don't worry about the reject pile for now. We'll get back to it.) When I was done, I had lunch and a drink. I needed it. When I had strength for it, I went back and once again tried on everything that I had put in the "Good Look Pile." This is where the buck stops—the end of the road. Only keep in that pile what you *can* and *will* wear happily and stylishly.

Now, I know this is the part where all you squirrels out there get nuts. "What?" you cry. "Get rid of this fabulous Giorgio Sant Angelo bodysuit that I bought in 1977 at 75 percent off?" I admit, I *was* hyperventilating when I got to this point in the process. But did I say that you had to get rid of *anything* permanently? No! *For now, make a pile of stuff that doesn't work.* I promise, you don't have to get rid of it! Just take some cardboard cartons (lots of them, probably) and start to put stuff there FOR THE TIME BEING.

STEP TWO: DECIDE ON A LOOK

So, now you've done a preliminary sort. Great. But difficult as it was, that isn't the hard part. Now you have to decide what you learned from your experience.

Believe me, it wasn't easy for me, and I certainly don't know what looks good on *you* (though Amy probably does). If *you* don't have a clue about what looks good on you, and what feels comfortable and what works in your life, you might need professional help. (More about that later.) I contend, however, that most of us *do* know, but we forget, or don't think about it, or get seduced when we shop. For most of us, it isn't a question of money or taste. It's really more a lack of focus. So take a long cool look at yourself. Remember Diana Vreeland's advice: "You've got to think of yourself and not how everyone else is dressed."

Robert Burns called it a gift only the gods could give us: to see yourself as others see you. Well, I have a sneaking suspicion that dour old Mr. Burns did not have *fashion* in mind when he penned those famous lines. But good poetry, like good wardrobe advice, always has a universal application, right?

So hold on to the Good Look Pile to assess again in the next chapter. Meanwhile . . .

STEP THREE: CONTEMPLATE THE TRAGEDIES

That scary bad pile has *got* to be addressed. Maybe, you think, there are treasures lurking there. Maybe you should keep it all. Well, not until you go through this process.

Get rid of the real mistakes. I'm embarrassed to admit that there were a few things with the price tags still on them. Good money paid, stuff never worn. If even Amy's done it, we've *all* done it. So be brave. Admit your worst mistakes. And try to see a pattern in your past errors. Courage. Remember the words of Georges Santayana: "Those that do not study history are condemned to repeat it."

Out with the things that don't fit. "It's nice but it always was too tight under the arms." Out! "I can't button the waist but I can wear an overblouse." Out! "It's pretty but I always have to pin the neckline or a breast falls out." Goodbye! And last, that terribly poignant, painful category: "Once I could fit into a size four. Maybe I will again." Ah! If only we could all be like Amy who's been the same size since she was fifteen. Well, forget about it. Get rid of it. When you hit size four again (dream on!), you have our permission to go on a shopping spree.

Out with the costumes. As Marcel Proust wrote, "Very few women are suited to old-fashioned dresses with an air of the theater or costume ball." Unless you've decided the costume look is absolutely you, get rid of the MGM casting wardrobe. I had to let go of two Victorian-looking white Laura Ashleys (I'm not sixteen anymore—or one hundred and ten pounds!), a Betsey Johnson black stretch floor-length witch dress (Halloween comes but once a year), a señorita crinoline (nice concept, but I bear *no* resemblance to Carmen Miranda), as well as an antique Japanese kimono jacket and an Indian fringed shawl. (At this point Amy became inspired too and made a museum donation of some vintage couture that had made her look like a Fifties fashion photo.) How does all this junk accumulate? The fact is, piece by piece, each of these has a certain charm. But can they be integrated into a workable, simple wardrobe? "*Non, non,*" as Marcel Proust might say.

I did have a co-worker, Mimi, who was a real character—a *different* character every day. One day she was an English schoolgirl, the next a biker babe, the next a southern belle with petticoats. It was interesting, but it was a full-time job and, not surprisingly, no one at our office ever took her seriously. Not to mention that she had to turn her entire apartment into a closet for her props and accessories. (She kept her shoes in the oven.) Needless to say, Mimi had no time for a real career. (She was working as a temp.) Unless you want to be Mimi, PUT THE COSTUMES IN A BOX.

Get rid of the sentimental favorites. Yeah, yeah, you wore it the night he proposed. But the marriage failed, it never looked good on you, it doesn't fit anymore, and it's *still* there, even though he isn't! Get rid of the prom dress, the sleepover camp T-shirt, the sorority sweater. "Is this a closet or a diary?" I asked myself. Have a separate box for these keepsakes, if you must. Think of them as memorabilia, not clothes. You may decide to keep them forever, but for now, out of your closet and into the box.

Unload those really expensive things that just don't work. I don't care if it's Versace and the most expensive skirt you ever bought—you look like a hippo in it, so put it aside. Somehow, the price ticket often makes us think we *should* wear something, even if it looks lousy. My favorite slacks of the universe were forty-nine dollars at The Gap. They're perfect, stylish and comfortable, and the designer version at four times the price never fit. (Amy got rid of some expensive Italian designer T-shirts with a badly cut V-neck and started wearing Hanes boys' T-shirts from Woolworth's instead.)

Okay. When I was done with this process I admit I was feeling lightheaded. I had filled six boxes. Take *your* boxes and put them out of sight. If you're feeling shaky and insecure—like someone in drug withdrawal—repeat to yourself, "I still have all my clothes, only they're not all in my closet."

STEP FOUR: FURTHER SORT THE GARMENTS FROM YOUR "KEEP" PILE

The aim here is to put the good stuff together into outfits. I decided on a general outfit as my best look: a blouse, jacket and narrow-legged pants. How did I decide? Here's a clue: I already had six of each. What do *you* keep buying and wearing? However, you, like me, will probably find that all tapered trousers were not created equal. This step is all about selectivity. And, to be honest, there *were* other things I liked. So, I went through the pile again and began yet another cleaning-out process. The point is to find your personal uniform.

If you find this difficult (my girlfriend, Janet, called up crying over this one) here are some basic guidelines:

Put aside stuff that you still like but that doesn't work with anything else. Who knows? You may decide later that the sophisticated knit suit *isn't* your basic unit, but for now, we're pretty convinced that those cowboy boots won't work with it. So put them in another box.

Out with the things that need fixing. There was this whole category of stuff that I didn't wear because: I lost an irreplaceable button, a zipper was broken, a back hem was coming down, jacket pockets were torn, a seam was opened, or needed to be taken up/let down/taken in/let out.

Some, I'm embarrassed to say, had been hanging like that for a long time (like half a decade for the Chanel-like sweater minus a Chanel-like button). But some, unfixed as they were, I loved and I decided they *were* part of my basic look. *So I fixed them* (see chapter 13). I mean, when you've got twenty pairs of assorted pants, there's no hurry to fix the broken zipper in one. When you pare down to six, there is. And then I didn't have that awful experience of getting dressed—only to find my pants were torn and I had to start over.

Now arrange the clothes into the best possible single combination. *Which* blouse with *which* pair of cropped pants? **Make outfits.** And if you find you have a bottom without a top or a dress that needs a jacket—hang it on the side. You'll have to get something that works with it or eliminate it. Arrange the rest of the closet.

Speaking of closets, step back and take a look at the little darling.

STEP FIVE: SURVEY WHAT YOU HAVE WROUGHT

Oh, my God! You're left with nothing to wear! At this point it is helpful to remember the immortal words of Chanel, "Simplicity doesn't mean poverty." Amy says that opening a closet door should be like arriving at a really good party where everyone you see is some-one you like. But now you will probably, if you're like me, also be panic-stricken when you look into your newly lean closet. It should be at least half as crowded as it was. But now it's organized by outfits. Complete units. Easy to see, easy to wear. I can get dressed in seven minutes. And *like* what I have on. In fact, I dress in half the time I used to and look twice as good. But:

Don't give/throw away anything yet. Who knows? You may have made a mistake. *Nothing* gets thrown away. Wait. After chapters 4, 5 and 6 you may want or need to go through the process again.

And if you *still* have nagging doubts about some of your remaining clothes, why not have a friend try some of them on so you can see how they look from a more objective perspective? Amy discovered through this method that some of her clothes that were *almost* right for her were actually *perfect* for her friend Miriam, who wears the same size and has a similar (but not identical) style. "It's happened more than once," Amy says. "The near misses in my closet are hits with my best friend. Now Miriam, her sister Vivian and I circulate clothes out of our closets to one another."

Organize what you've got. You know how to do this: slacks in one section, blouses in another, skirts in a third, etc. Right? *Wrong!* Only closet salesmen will push this on you. Although America is the land of "coordinates" and "separates" I've found these pieces often don't coordinate and usually *stay* separate. All beige blouses *don't* go with all grey skirts. So, try to arrange complete units: blouse with slacks with belt with scarf with jacket. All together. Ready to grab and put on at a moment's notice. Yes, you do lose some flexibility but, if you've done your homework, what you gain is your ultimate, most polished looks. (And if dresses are your uniform, you're way ahead of the game.)

What did *I* wind up with? Don't—*please* don't—use this as a guide for yourself. Remember, I'm a childless forty-year-old writer who spends 80 percent of her life at home and 20 percent with my publishers or on book tours. *My* list is only that. Mine. With that said, here's what can be found in my lean closet:

I decided to use black or dark slacks as my foundation piece in a variety of fabrics for traveling. I have silk, wool, a tuxedo stripe, and cotton/spandex Gap pants that fit like a dream.

I have a couple of straight cut and one pleated skirt for more dressy occasions.

My assortment of blouses are all white, beige or taupe and are mostly silk. Okay, I admit it: I'm a silk shirt–aholic. So lock me up! But it is *my* uniform, and you can only wear 'em once before washing or cleaning them. I have just two patterned blouses that go with almost all the slacks, but I did pair them up into outfits as alternatives to the plain blouses.

I am partial to long blazers (they cover the hips) and I choose to have them in neutrals.

As for my handknit sweaters, I couldn't give them *all* up, could I? And I wear them when a blazer is too formal.

This gives you an idea of how much I had before I started simplifying! I think I can do with less, but so far this is really working for me. But please, don't pattern yourself on my wardrobe. This isn't about copying, it's about *evolving*.

STEP SIX: LEARN THE ZEN PHILOSOPHY OF FASHION

This is the really important part. Remember the words of Diana Vreeland: "Elegance is refusal." If you don't get this you're doomed to repeat the cycle over and over again, moving through malls in a fog, restocking your closets, a slave to the evil garmentos, lost forever in fashion purgatory, reincarnated again and again. When I shop do I still look at the marked-down, lime green raw silk jacket with the polka dot rosette? Or the orange suede swing coat? I admit I linger over them longingly—and then I leave 'em! I *have* changed the way I dress and the way I shop. Bob Mackie put it well: "Too many women follow the fashion. You'd do better to stick with a style and only add a piece or two a year." So, look in the mirror and repeat your first fashion mantra:

MANTRA 1: *I want to look stylish. To do it, I must keep things simple.*

Princess Di can have an outfit for every occasion but she's had an (almost) unlimited budget and a staff of three who clean and press and sort and hang her clothes. And it was her *job* to change her clothes twelve times a day!

So now take a deep breath and repeat your second, third and fourth mantras:

MANTRA 2: *A full closet does not mean stylish.*

MANTRA 3: *Shopping all the time does not mean stylish.*

MANTRA 4: *Changing my look every season (or month, or week, or day!) does not mean stylish.*

Repeat these mantras twenty-five thousand times. Repeat them as you read a fashion magazine at the dentist's. Repeat them as you walk past department store windows. Repeat them as you go through the rest of this sorting-out process.

STEP SEVEN: PRACTICE WEARING THIS STUFF FOR A MONTH

With my new, pared down, only-the-best closet I immediately found it easier and more fun to dress. In the past, as I told you, I'd begin by selecting a skirt or dress or pair of slacks. Then I'd get confused as I scanned the whole closet for the blouse or jacket or sweater to go with it. Now I simply pick a whole outfit. And that gives me the luxury of time to think about the telling details. A black jeweled belt and matching socks. Or a chunky chain and a glint of Lurex stocking underneath. I'm looking good. Honestly!

Progress Report

It is now seven months into my *Simple Isn't Easy* approach to style. I know that I spend less time dressing and I also believe I look a lot more stylish. It's a discipline I can keep to, with a few slips and corrections. My sister even asked me, "You look so nice lately. Have you lost weight?"

Bingo!

SELF-ASSESSMENT

or

Mirror, Mirror on the Wall

> "Know yourself, then create yourself."
> —Mary McFadden

> "It is as hard to see one's self as to look backwards without turning around."
> —Henry David Thoreau

Well, you've cleaned out your closet and you feel better for it, but how are you sure you've selected the real "you"? I was lucky. I had Amy's help. But how do you do it? As Teilhard de Chardin said, "The whole of life lies in the verb *seeing*." Really looking at yourself is a difficult skill to learn. Most of us tend to be either too self-critical or to ignore the "problem areas" we ought to deal with. Both are deadly. So let us share the secret of style self-discovery. It's called a mirror.

Goethe wrote that "thinking is more interesting than knowing, but less interesting than looking." This chapter is all about looking and learning to see. Can you imagine that mirrors did not begin to become widely available until the Seventeenth century? (Do you now wish that you could time travel back to a no-mirror world? Then you *really* need to pay attention to this chapter.) There is no escaping your reflection. Even the beautiful Narcissus of Greek mythology managed to find a lake to look into so he could fall in love with himself. (Unfortunately a lot of these Narcissus guys are still alive and walking amongst us. In fact, I think I saw one last night at my neighborhood bistro, ignoring his date and preening in the looking glass.) We are not encouraging empty vanity here, but realistic self-awareness. Remember, even if there were a law against mirrors, your reflection would still be everywhere. It is in the effect you make on other people, from perfect strangers to imperfect husbands. And, as the Italian designer Gianni Versace recognized, "A woman today still likes to show herself off, to please both herself and a man."

We should be grateful for the modern world's technological self-reflecting wonders: mirrors, cameras and video recorders. Because through these devices we are going to learn to assess ourselves clinically and objectively, so that we may never fear a camera or mirror—or the gaze of another's eyes—again.

Mirrors

Consider your mirror not as an enemy but as your strongest ally. No fooling. It has traits that even your best friend might lack. It never tells you you're looking good when you're not, nor will it enviously tell you you look bad (or that euphemism "tired") when you don't. Why is it that Amy's baby girl, Flora, knows instinctively that the mirror is her friend, while we grown-up women don't? When Flora sees her reflection she grins and laughs at her image and strokes the glass with pleasure—sometimes she even kisses it! Weren't we all like that once? What happened? Our guess is that somewhere along the way we've developed some ideal that we aspire to—suggested by movies, ads, boyfriends, parents, etc.—and that most often this just doesn't correspond with what we see looking back at us.

In our self-assessment plan, you'll either: lose that old counterproductive ideal and replace it with another; fulfill your ideal (or a realistic facsimile); or accept yourself exactly as you are and become comfortable and happy with that image. It is necessary, though difficult, to achieve one of these states of being because otherwise you (and I) are doomed to external dissatisfaction. And it all begins with self-assessment.

The most important step for self-assessment is to set up some full-length mirrors **permanently** in your house that give you a **front, side and back view of yourself.** *Of all the suggestions we have to offer in this book, this one might rank as number one.* We are not paper dolls with only one frontal view (even if you want to be!). Close your eyes and for a second picture your mother, your child or someone else you see often. I guarantee that you did not think of them face-on with their arms dropped stiffly to their sides, but in movement, from an angle. Well, for better or worse, that is how the rest of the world pictures *and* sees you. Clothes should be a moving, fluid, three-dimensional part of that picture. As Yves Saint Laurent put it, "I like to watch the way a model moves in my clothes, the way she gives them life, or if they are wrong, stillborn, the way her life rejects them."

When they see a woman dressed inappropriately for her age, her figure or the occasion, all the fashion designers Amy knows make the same remark: "Did she look in the mirror before she went out?" Similarly, Graydon Carter, the dapper editor-in-chief of *Vanity Fair* magazine, quips, "If people *really* studied themselves in a three-way mirror you'd see a lot less spandex on the street." Sonia Rykiel adds that her most basic style advice to a woman is "to stay one, two, four hours, one, two, fifteen days, a month in front of the mirror to make sure she knows what does and doesn't suit her."

Now, that isn't meant to scare you or make you feel you must dress to please either fashion pros or magazine editors. We're only asking you to *see* yourself clearly and then make the decision about how you want to be seen. You don't have to please everyone, but you ought to be aware of how you look, and how you look to others. Then decide how you want to present yourself. As Bill Blass told us, "Follow your own instincts and not friends or books." Except ours!

So, be courageous! Stand before your three-way mirror in a leotard, your bra and underpants or—if you can bear it—in the nude. (Consider this old French saying: "Women dress well in countries where they undress often.")

See your total being, now, not just the parts. Yes, women *are* objectified by society and by themselves as well, but remember how many different parts of that "object"—yourself—there are. If an artist were to paint a full-length portrait of you, do you think she would just look at your bust, your waist, your hips, your face and your hair? Of course not—she would scrutinize all that lay in between (your ankle bones, your fingers, the curve of your shoulder, the shape of your earlobes). So why reduce yourself to the sum of a few parts? Almost every woman we know—no matter her shape or weight or age—hates her thighs and thinks her bust is either too large or too small. Forget those most obvious categories and see the whole. Your "measurements" are not a tripartite sum—even a tailor knows that. So what if a beauty pageant director doesn't!

Remember, too, no one is consistently perfect, or consistently imperfect everywhere. I was so saddened to read in Gloria Steinem's memoir that the *only* part she liked about herself was her hands. They are indeed lovely, but so is so much else. So focus not just on the obvious—those parts that we typically obsess over—like thighs and breasts and buttocks. Think of the *whole picture*.

Also bear in mind that adopting good posture can make your whole physical presence more attractive. You'd be surprised how many "flaws" improve when you stand the way a dancer does, with chest high, head straight on, and back straight. It will at least give you the illusion of confidence and poise—not to mention that clothes will also hang better on you!

To help you discover your whole self as well as neglected parts of your anatomy, which may in fact be points of beauty, and to help you see yourself in a new, more enlightened way, we've devised a self-assessment chart (see page 54). Rate yourself, as you stand before your mirror, for the body parts we listed. And learn to play up with your clothes the parts that you love. Simply cover, minimize or ignore those parts you don't. *That's* what clothes are for!

Now ask yourself these questions:

Do you love everything you see? (If the answer is a resounding "yes," you may have bought the wrong book. You can wear anything!) If your answer is "no," proceed with the following:

What do you like best about what you see? (Your long neck, your shapely calves, your full cleavage, your height, etc.) These are your strong points, the ones you'll want your clothes to emphasize. And you *do* have *some*. Focus on the positive.

What do you like least? (Your short neck, your shapeless calves, your bony cleavage, your height, etc.) These aren't tragedies; they are merely target areas that you want clothes to camouflage or minimize.

Don't stop yet! The operation is painful but you'd have a quadruple bypass to save your heart, wouldn't you? This is only slightly more painful, and hey, at least nobody is watching you.

You don't need Amy's fashion savvy to tell you to accentuate the positive and change, minimize or ignore the negative, do you? (And I hope all your

Amy and Olivia's

Positive Assessment List

FEATURE	LOVE IT	DON'T LIKE IT	NEUTRAL
Ears			
Jawline			
Neck			
Shoulders			
Back—upper			
Upper arms			
Lower arms			
Wrists			
Hands			
Knees			
Ankles			
Feet			
Back—lower			
Ribs			
Calves			
Abdomen			
Forehead			
Head shape			
Collarbone			
Profile			
Pelvis			
Backbone			

Accentuate the Positive!

check marks aren't in the middle column. If you hate yourself that much, you need more than wardrobe counseling.) Sonia Rykiel's wisdom here is important to remember: She told us that the single thing that destroys or diminishes a woman is "not to love oneself, not to admire oneself in the mirror." Let that be your goal.

So, as the doctor says to the patient, "All right. You can get dressed now." Please put on a couple of your favorite ensembles from your closet, and stand again before your three-way, full-length mirror. You've already decided that you like the way these outfits look on you. Now, based on your self-assessment, can you analyze why?

If you're happy with what a particular outfit does for you, it's probably because it enhances something (you named it above) that you like about yourself, or minimizes something you're not crazy about in yourself. For example, Amy loves a dress she owns (in both a summer and a winter version) because it's got built-into-the-seams curves, which somehow make her straight-up-and-down figure seem like an hourglass. Her friend Rebecca loves nothing better than long, straight dresses. Why? Her weak point, she feels, is her legs, which are thick and straight. Yet her hips are slim. The long-line dresses show off what she's decided is appealing, while making what she doesn't like less noticeable.

There are no rules here. You must figure out what works best for *you*, and makes *you* happy. But **don't**

lie to yourself or make excuses you don't believe in. Be courageous, yet gentle. Emanuel Ungaro says women's most common mistake is "following trends blindly and not looking at themselves in the mirror with a critical yet kind eye."

One last mirror suggestion: When you check out your outfit in front of your mirror before you leave the house, move, bend and turn a bit. Don't stand like a wax-works display. That way you'll see if the dress's wrap sash starts to come undone, or the seam of the seat of your pants starts to ride up. And you'll see yourself more as you really *are*—really the key to this exercise. Remember the advice Sonia Rykiel gave us. She believes what gives a woman style is, "The way she walks, the way she stands. The art of dressing with regards to her body." It's about movement.

Cameras and Video Recorders

Talk about seeing yourself as you really are, how about looking over whatever snapshots and videos have been taken of you recently? I know—the camera adds ten pounds and you never took a good picture. But study photos differently this time. Instead of hiding away the ones you hate and gazing with satisfaction at the ones you like, look more deeply. What is it that you really liked about that picture of you at your best friend's third wedding? Do you love the way that little ribboned hat set off your large brown eyes? The way that red polka dot scarf brought a rosy glow to your skin? The way the long dark sleeves of your dress accentuated your pretty, expressive hands?

What is it that made you shriek in horror at the family Christmas video tapes? (Besides your mother-in-law's turkey?) Was it the sight of your belly bulging under your flowered silk dress? The cloud of frizz that you thought was your hairdo?

Always question the *reasons* for your reactions to your own image. If you can identify a reaction and name the problem that caused it, then you can solve it if you want to. Incorporate the good looks into your daily wardrobe. Permanently drop the bad ones.

Use your camera, like your mirror, as an ally. It is a tool for accurate self-assessment and can point the way to whatever change you would like to see in yourself. Here are a couple of exercises you can do with your Instamatic or video camera:

Exercise One

Get together with a friend, and have her take pictures of you in different outfits. (Amy did this with me and a Polaroid.) Talk, walk, move, sit, turn, bend, etc. Study the results. Again, decide what you like and what you don't, and analyze why. **Always ask why.** You can try this experiment another way without an accomplice:

Exercise Two

At the next event when a camera is called for, have someone take the usual casual, friendly snapshots or videos. You will notice (now that you will be analyzing the results with a more enlightened, concentrated purpose), that you are a bit more self-conscious about how you look, how you behave and how you want to be seen. This is good. If you find yourself feeling like a performer, remember you are your own audience. **Turn your self-consciousness into self-awareness.** This will help as you evaluate the results of the photo session.

"Every eye is a mirror." This is a line written by Gloria Vanderbilt (who, Amy says, is one of the most sensational-looking women she has ever seen). She is a woman who has such self-awareness and assurance that she never seems to think about her own appearance. This complete sense of herself allows her to concentrate her attentions solely on whomever she is with, and that—not her considerable natural beauty—is the secret of her charm. For our purposes, we will extend Gloria's phrase to say that **"Every eye is also a camera."** Though the exercises you practiced at home may seem artificial and contrived, they are really a private enactment of what takes place every day on the street, in the mall, at work, at the grocery store, whether you like it or not! People—strangers, friends and family—notice you wherever you go. We want you to feel *good* about that.

Emanuel Ungaro told us, "A woman with an 'allure' is one that knows herself, is in charge of her sensuality and uses the right tools to seduce."

But if, despite help from mirrors and cameras, you *still* have trouble seeing yourself clearly and objectively, or if you need an aid to guide you from your household mirror out into the theater of life, here's a small suggestion: Imagine, as you're getting dressed in front of the mirror, and then as you go out and participate in the world, that there's a single, benevolent eye watching you. How do you look to this eye? You can think of it as a guardian angel, or an exterior part of your consciousness—whatever helps. This eye cares about you, but doesn't lie.

And here are some important parting thoughts from Amy that both of us have profited from:

What You've Been Told Are Your Defects May in Fact Be Your Strongest Points

Don't believe what you've been told by your family or your old boyfriends. Did it ever occur to you they may not always have your best interests at heart? "Flap Ears, Skinny Minnie, Stick" are all names Amy heard growing up. Well, guess what? After years of hiding her ears, hating her weight, downplaying her height, etc., Amy now *accentuates* those features. As a reedy 5'10" teenager she feared heels. To exaggerate her deviation from the norm seemed terrifying. Then her uncle Ray pointed out that high heels would increase her height by a smaller percentage than they would on a petite girl. Ever since, Amy has gloried in the extra height heels allow. Go for it.

Make Your Imperfections Your Trademarks

Truman Capote, who knew more about beautiful women than they know about themselves, invented a character in *Breakfast at Tiffany's* called Mag Wildwood. She was too tall, too clumsy, too flat-chested, and she stammered—but she was a drop-dead gorgeous, highly sought-after model. The secret of her extraordinary glamour? She exaggerated each of her shortcomings so that they became her charms.

Celebrities know how to exploit their physical irregularities. What would Barbra Streisand be without her nose, Anna Nicole Smith without her larger-than-life bod or Dolly Parton without her white-trash glamour? (As Dolly says, "It takes a lot of money to look this cheap!") Strangely enough, what you dislike in yourself may be exactly what others yearn for. I know an exercise instructor named Suzy who hates her pronounced jaw because her husband always makes fun of it. My reaction: "What I wouldn't give for a strong jawline!" It certainly never stopped Jacqueline Kennedy from being beautiful. As Francis Bacon wrote, "There is no beauty without some strangeness in its proportions."

It Is Seldom a Good Idea to Go Against the Grain and Force Yourself to Be the Opposite of What You Are

After all, it never worked for Cinderella's ugly stepsisters: Her dainty glass slipper still didn't fit. A straight-haired brunette seldom makes a good curly-haired blonde. Wonderbras and peplum waists will never turn a rail-thin waif into a Marilyn Monroe bombshell. An exotic-looking dark-skinned woman will rarely seem right dressed like a Connecticut WASP. These attempts at an ego about-face are generally recipes for unhappiness. As the Greek philosopher Epictetus said, "Know, first, who you are; and then dress accordingly."

Change What You Can

If you are truly miserable about certain aspects of yourself, if your posture, your thighs, your nose, your teeth are impossible to live with, don't pretend they're not a problem or decide there's nothing you can do. *Don't be defeated.* Go to an exercise specialist, a reputable (this is *very* important) plastic surgeon or cosmetic dentist. Go on a diet and stick with it. You *can* alter your fate. No one else can do that for you. (I've lost fourteen pounds since I started writing this book!)

Liberate Yourself From Those Wretched Little Rules That Strait-Jacket You

Suppress the noises made by that nasty little "shouldn't" voice inside of you. It is the voice of self-loathing and fear. "Redheads shouldn't wear pink," "You're too skinny to wear black," "You're too fat to wear stripes," "You're too busty to wear knits," "You shouldn't mix greens and pinks because they clash." We believe that if you love a color you should wear it. *And that style often lies in the reversal of these rules.* A redhead *can* look fabulous in pink, and if you love your big bustline, why not show it off?

Abandon Your Fears, Your Denials, the Little Lies You Tell Yourself.

Be good to yourself. Be honest. Otherwise you are sleepwalking through life and will never be happy with the way you look (or with anything else). Lying to yourself is crippling. This is not a dress rehearsal. This is your life.

I can't tell you how you want to look or what works for you and neither can a magazine, your husband or your mother. It's something you have to decide for yourself. As Fleur Cowles, painter, writer and founder of *FLAIR* magazine, told Amy, "Decide how you want to be seen, and look like that." But what if *you* still can't decide? If you're sixteen, you probably *shouldn't* yet know how you want to look. But if, like me, you're a baby boomer, the time may have come to take control of this whole fashion thing once and for all. You may get lucky as I did, and find that your closet reveals yourself to you. But if it hasn't yet, there is still hope! Move on to the next chapter.

Q&A Designer

Q: What is the most common wardrobe mistake you see women commit?

A: Not understanding proportions.

—*Mary McFadden*

COMFORT vs. STYLE

or

The Balancing Act

> "It is only shallow people
> who do not judge by appearances."
> —Oscar Wilde

From a modern perspective, the contraptions that women have been forced to wear in the name of style—corsets, stays, steel hoops, girdles—all seem like torture devices. It's hard to think of a single female garment that existed between the Roman toga and the flapper's shift that appears comfortable by contemporary standards. But, strangely enough, women during all these long centuries never really complained about being uncomfortable. Diaries from the Nineteenth century even reveal that some women *liked* the sensation of being tight-laced. Health issues aside, what does this tell us?

Comfort is as much a state of mind as a physical reality.

Comfort is what a culture agrees upon as comfort. For example, up until the Seventeenth century, nobody in the western world even had upholstered furniture in their houses. Yet before padded furniture nobody thought hard, upright wooden chairs were a problem.

When Sixties feminists discarded their bras to celebrate their new freedom their gesture only made symbolic sense. Just ask any size 36D woman—she'll tell you she'd be less comfortable braless than Jackie Joyner-Kersee would be running a race in platforms.

A male reporter once asked Amy what was the most comfortable garment ever designed, and she proposed the caftan. The next thing she knew he had gone into a closet and donned a caftan Amy's husband had brought back from Morocco years ago. And what do you think his assessment was? He felt uncomfortable, of course, because to him it felt like he had on a dress! (Just as well. He didn't really have the figure for it.)

Actually, *I'm* not comfortable in a caftan either, because I hate the sensation of my own bare skin rubbing against itself—that's why I like slacks. I feel strangled in a turtleneck; they make Amy feel secure. Anyway, from all these disparate viewpoints we have learned that as far as comfort today goes, one woman's meat is another woman's poison. *But comfort is also tied to appropriateness*, the socially accepted standards of the moment—that men (usually) don't wear dresses, and that businesswomen at work don't wear black nipple-baring bras showing under their white silk blouses. The good news is:

Comfort and style are not necessarily contradictory states of being. In fact they can be closely related.

If you don't *somehow* resemble your peers in the shop, office, or the classroom, you're probably not going to be comfortable.

Don't think the ultimate comfort is nudity. How comfortable are *you* stark naked? See what we mean?

Today most of our ideas about comfort in clothing come from leisure and sports clothes. When women want to "slip into something more comfortable" these days, they don't mean a marabou-trimmed Jean Harlow satin nightie. Most women reach for those worn leggings, a T-shirt, and a pair of sneakers. I'm probably most comfortable in my old sweat pants, Nike Air Max and a soft flannel shirt. For Amy, it would be her white Fernando Sanchez bathrobe and leopard mules. (This is why we both live in fear of video telephones.) But, comfortable as we are that way, if we suddenly had to appear on a TV talk show, how comfortable would we be in our so-called "most comfortable" outfits?

Let's examine, for a moment, the widely held conviction that jeans—that universal symbol of American democratic style and the most successful single garment of the Twentieth century—are a comfortable article of clothing. Oh, yeah? What about that tendency they have of biting your crotch? Ouch!! Or gapping at the waist, or pulling across your thighs. The fabric is rough (though appealingly durable), the seams are thick, lumpy, and heavy as canned ravioli. They're too warm for the summer, and too cool for the winter. Think about it. Both Amy and I believe it's next to impossible to find a pair that fits well. And it's definitely not the best look on most women—though there may be some lovely exceptions (Amy can think of only two: her rangy, athletic friend Alison and Annie Oakley). So what's the deal?

Our theory is that jeans fit the current *image* of what's carefree and casual. They are a secure choice: After all, *everyone* wears them, from movie stars to the kid at the car wash. They're democratic. So you feel *secure* in your garment—but not necessarily comfortable. Be conscious. Jeans as comfortable wear are a myth we all bought! Now, understand, we're not saying "Don't wear jeans." We're only pointing out they may not be as *comfortable* a choice as you thought. And that many of our beliefs are illusions.

Sneakers, except for maybe old-fashioned Keds, are, in their way, more unattractive on the foot than jeans are on the imperfect butt. Modern athletic shoes are clumsy, goofy, graceless (aren't those names of the Seven Dwarfs?). And they're deadly with a suit or dress. (Amy even refuses to wear them at her exercise class! "I go barefoot," she says. "After all, I'm from Tennessee!") So why do we as a nation cling to them? Ask anyone, and they'll name comfort as the reason. Then why isn't every foot in the nation shod in orthopedic shoes instead? The answer is that Granny's podiatrically correct clodhoppers are linked in everyone's minds with infirmity, while Nikes, Reeboks, etc., connote health and youth.

Here's another way of demonstrating the surprisingly wide-ranging feelings about comfort: During Amy's pregnancy, when her preoccupation with comfort was heightened, she felt most at ease in a trapeze dress and sandals. But her friend Martine detested the idea of a dress, and instead lived for nine months in leggings and smock-style blouses. When Amy tried out leggings, she found they bound her knee constricted her circulation and cut into her stomach. *Comfort, girls, is relative—relative to your own tastes, relative to the situation you're in, and relative to the period in which you are living.* So think about the roles you play in your life, and the clothes you need for them: Try not to polarize your wardrobe into comfortable vs. stylish clothes—the jogging suit and sneakers vs. the itchy cocktail dress that cuts into your waist. Life shouldn't be reduced to the worn denims vs. the stiff business suit.

What we are suggesting you aim for is an approach that doesn't make you uncomfortable, nor does it leave you inappropriately underdressed. To do this successfully means you must have an awareness of your own physical comfort as well as your lifestyle.

It's too bad we don't all have the time, talent and liberty to re-invent clothes for ourselves. Geoffrey Beene, who believes the male uniform of suit and tie is obsolete, now only wears a jacket of his own devising. It is simply a man's suit jacket transformed by being made of a soft knit jersey fabric instead of a woven gabardine or flannel. "It has the comfort of a cardigan, but the propriety of a suit jacket," he explains. Comfort and style!

This is the kind of resolution of opposites we aim for. So, to review, when you think about your clothes and your wardrobe in the next chapters, remember that:

Comfort is partly a state of mind—not body—that can vary from one individual to another, one situation to another, one time period to another.

Style does not necessarily contradict comfort—it can enhance it.

A woman of style is never uncomfortable in her clothes. She feels as good in her dinner suit as she does in her gardening clothes.

As designer Betsy Gonzalez said, "A woman should never wear anything she can't do the Mambo in."

You can probably find both comfort and style in your own closet.

In the words of Yves Saint Laurent, "Finding your own style is not easy, but once found brings complete happiness. It gives you self-confidence, always." Now we're going to help you do that.

WEIGHT A MINUTE!

or

A Waist Is a Terrible Thing to Mind

> "There is nothing either good or bad
> but thinking makes it so."
> —Shakespeare

I could be (and have been) called "plump," "rounded," "pudgy," "zaftig," and simply "overweight." What I am is average. I am five foot four (statistically average height for an American woman) and, as I began to write this book, I weighed one hundred and forty-six pounds—exactly average. (Now that is a sentence that takes courage to write!) So, at average height and weight for an American woman, why is it that I feel so much shorter and fatter?

Statistics indicate that *all* Americans (not just me and you) gain a little weight each year from the time they are thirty. Having hit forty (and having sat on my, shall we say, "chair" for four years working on my last three novels), I find myself more of a broad than ever before. But I am not alone.

Overall, a third of the adult population, some fifty-eight million Americans, is overweight, up from a quarter of the population just fifteen years ago. According to the *Annals of Internal Medicine,* most dieters manage to lose only 10 percent of the weight they hoped to—and, as most of us know from experience, even *that* doesn't stay off. The same report shows that one-third to two-thirds of dieters regain the weight within a year; just about all of it is back on within five years.

I always mean to lose weight. I exercise regularly and I haven't had a dessert (not even my own birthday cake) in the last two years. The fact is, sometimes I *am* ten pounds slimmer, but I'm still not happy because I long to be the hundred and twenty-one pounds I was at my college graduation. So for quite a few years I didn't make the best of myself because I was waiting for the magic to happen—I was waiting to be thin again.

WELL, I'M NOT WAITING ANY LONGER AND I DON'T THINK YOU SHOULD EITHER. The fact is, recent surveys reveal that more than 80 percent of us believe we are overweight (and that includes adolescent girls and anorectics). Amy—who is five foot ten and whose weight barely gets out of the double digits—watches her eating as carefully as I watch mine. Susie Orbach had it right when she wrote *Fat Is a Feminist Issue:* We are a nation of females obsessed with eating and weight loss. So I'm here to tell you once again that *your weight—whatever it is—is no excuse to put off putting together a wardrobe that is as flattering and comfortable as possible.*

I know that's hard. I refused to shop if I couldn't fit into "my" old size, so I wore things that I could barely button and that looked awful on me. Or I wore sweat pants and a sloppy shirt to "hide" my weight. Well, it didn't hide anything, especially my lack of self-esteem and style. Garmentos have taken advantage of our obsession and shame over weight by their practice of "downsizing": enlarging size standards so that we can fool ourselves into thinking we're a 10. We haven't lost an ounce or an inch, but our vanity is touched and our wallet is emptied just because a maker put a size 10 label on his size 12 or 14. And not only raw civilians like you or I are flattered, so was Eleanor Lambert. "I was so proud that I wore an eight at Halston. But I think it was a twelve marked eight."

Many of us fool ourselves by thinking that in just a week, a month, or a year we'll be thin and perfect and that until then it's useless to try and look good. Don't fall for that kind of denial. Right now, today, your life is taking place and—at whatever weight you are—there's no excuse not to try to look as attractive as you can. *Carpe diem.* Seize the day. There are several reasons to do it.

Looking Good—at Any Weight—*Is* Possible

Giorgio Armani told us that "chic bones," meaning thin ankles and wrists, long neck and high cheekbones, etc., is one of the greatest gifts mother nature can give a woman. But he went on to say, "This doesn't mean that women who aren't blessed with a perfect figure shouldn't have style!" As he explained it, "Style is something that comes from within." I am not so optimistic or stupid as to say that a three-hundred-pounder can look just like Cheryl Tiegs. But we all watched Delta Burke wax and wane on *Designing Women*, and there wasn't a time when she didn't look well-groomed and put together. Her clothes fit properly, which did a lot to make her look attractive. She had—and has—her own style and panache, no matter what she tipped the scales at. And we all loved her for it. Once, in India, I attended a business party with several male co-workers. The belle of the ball was a middle-aged Hindu woman in a sari. She was a dozen years older and easily outweighed me by fifty pounds, but there was something about her that kept the men entranced. She had charm and confidence. Later, when I asked one of the men about his reaction to her, he got a surprised look on his face and said, "She was irresistible. She was so very self-assured and sensual." He confided in me that he thought she was very sexy. And she was old enough to be his mother. Now, I am not saying that it is easy in *our* society for a *so-called* overweight woman to exude self-confidence, but it can be done. *New York* magazine ran a fashion feature on style writer Mary Martz. In her thirties she decided to "work *with*" her weight. "And I never shopped in a fat-lady store." She looks terrific. And looking terrific makes you feel terrific. When you feel good you take better care of yourself.

Looking Bad Demoralizes You

The surest way to gain more weight is to play ostrich, put your head in the sand and just hope the problem goes away. The other mistake is to give up. When I was in my sweat suit mode, even a glance at my reflection would make me feel so bad about myself that I would sit down and polish off a couple of Devil Dogs. Looking bad is a kind of self-punishment that only increases your humiliation and self-hatred. Right now, today, get dressed comfortably and attractively in clothes that *fit* you, whatever your size. Finally . . .

Dressing Well and Looking Good May Actually Motivate You to Lose Weight

Don't believe that if you collect a beautiful wardrobe in size 14 you will be stuck there forever. When I dropped a size because of my exercise program, I didn't hesitate to have my slacks altered and go out and buy a few nice new things in size 10. What a triumph.

Please notice that I am *not* suggesting a diet program or some magic weight-loss exercise and eating regime. I say live in the present, whatever weight you are. Dress to camouflage those parts you are least happy with and to emphasize those parts you like best. Also remember that you are not alone. There have been so many diet books printed that if I merely weight lifted all of the ones I've bought I'd be as slim as Amy or Kate Moss. Nowadays we are all so infected with the anti-fat virus that the thinnest adolescent girls complain about their imaginary fat thighs while otherwise contented, attractive matrons long to regain their adolescent bodies. Once again, we can look to European women who, when they reach a certain age, neither try to emulate teenagers *nor* give up and sink into an elastic-waisted skirt and an oversized man's shirt. They dress well and appropriately and I try to do the same. And one advantage of a bit of fat is that it does soften the facial features. As a famous French beauty (who had, with age, put on some weight but few wrinkles) said, "It's either my face or my ass!" So I struggle to stay in my size, look good and like who I am. (By the way, I have barely a wrinkle on my pudgy, over-forty face!)

7

STRATEGIES

or

Six Never-Fail Fixes

> "Our life is frittered away by detail . . .
> Simplify, simplify."
> —Henry David Thoreau

Okay, so now you've assessed what you have in your closet and what you look like in your clothes, but maybe you're still not certain about how to put together a "look." What choices of a uniform are there if you haven't found one? So presented below are six never-fail fixes. One of them just may make sense for you.

1. Use a Single Color

Priscilla, a big, tall, Texas blonde, wears virtually any silhouette, from a minidress to a formal suit—as long as the outfit is red. "Valentine red makes me happy," she explains. "And I get my variety in wearing my skirts slim or bouffant, or wearing slacks and sweaters or any shape I want to. It's just all in red. It's become my trademark, in a way. All my friends give me red gifts. My little sister does the same with cotton-candy pink."

This single-color strategy is especially common in the fashion world, though there the color of choice is most often black (a gathering of designers, models, and editors could be mistaken for a pallbearers' convention). Why black? Because almost all blacks go together—not to mention the fact that that day's stains and wrinkles seem to disappear, and that black is always slimming. Also, black has been perceived as chic since before Chanel invented the little black

dress. "Black is not a trend. It's there forever," says
Geoffrey Beene.

But remember that there is a complication in the one-
color strategy: not all oranges are created equal. Nor
is the one color that you have chosen always going to
be available. One reason why the monochrome look
is most popular with red, black, white, beige or navy is
because these colors are fashion perennials and
almost always offered each season. Even if a color is
meant to be consistent, dye lots change from bolt to
bolt and season to season. Certain colors are
deemed to be "in" by the garmentos one season only
to disappear by the next one. If you've settled on
your favorite shade, just be warned that color is sometimes harder to match than to contrast or combine.

2. Stick With the Perennial Fashion Colors

As mentioned above, this is another color-based
fashion strategy. Use black, white, red, beige and
navy. You can build a wardrobe just on mixing these
five colors and add from the best of any new season's offering, secure in the knowledge that they will
mix well together.

3. Select a Single Silhouette
and Stick With It

This one is tricky, since we know all too well that
silhouettes change faster than leaves in autumn.

Mary, Amy's friend, is arrestingly chic at age eighty and has been wearing the same dress for decades. Boy, does she look great in it. No, not just one dress, silly! A whole *closet* full of jewel-necked, long-sleeved, knee-length chemises that she sews herself, copied after one very costly original purchased way back in the mists of time. Amy's seen it in fluttering light silk in the summer, thick nubby tweed in the winter and it never ceases to impress. Mary not only found her style at an early age, but had the courage, savvy and spirit to stick with it.

A friend of mine bypasses retail establishments altogether. Tomboy-casual yet well-groomed, Jan wears either jeans and cardigan sweaters she handknits, or suits made by her husband's tailor, "always cut from the same pattern. And cheaper than lots of off-the-rack women's suits."

Sophia Loren has her own bifurcated version of this strategy. "I like classic clothes for day, but when I go out at night I like fluffy evening dresses. When you walk in one you feel like you are conquering the world." Well, it works for her. I'd feel silly and self-conscious in a huge taffeta skirt. But hey, she's got her (two) uniforms and I've got mine.

4. Stick With a Single Designer

There are times when that rare miracle occurs. You try on a dress or a pantsuit and you know—it was made for you. It fits *everywhere,* it flatters, it feels good. You want to wear it out of the shop and never take it off. You want to sleep and shower in it. Who designed it? What's on the label? Thank the maker. If you're lucky (and the designer is good) it will be like coming home every time you slip on his clothes.

Diana Vreeland, while fashion editor of *Harper's Bazaar,* had the opportunity to wear anything in the world—but day in and out she wore only Mainbocher suits. She found a designer, she found a uniform, and she looked divine. In fact, she became a legend.

Cynthia Carter, wife of *Vanity Fair* editor-in-chief Graydon, has a completely different look which also transcends fashion. For her it is about masses of dark curly hair, pale skin, and romantic, layered ensembles by Romeo Gigli. No one else looks like her, but everyone else looks *at* her—admiringly.

Amy also wholeheartedly embraces this monogamous fashion philosophy, in her clothes (Beene), her pantyhose (Hanes), and even her exercise wear (Gilda Manx). She finds this strictness about her choices liberating.

But buyer beware: With Seventh Avenue pattern makers, fit models and fabricators changing as often as your underwear and design teams large enough to fill a football stadium, consistency in a given label is rare and should be valued. When it's found, be faithful.

5. Stick With a Single Outfit in Every Color Available

Geoffrey Beene's design assistant tells us his most fashion savvy clients often purchase the same outfit in every color available, rather than buying all over the entire collection. The manager of one chic shoe boutique in New York says that her most well-shod customers do the same with their favorite pumps or boots. I myself have the same pair of terrific lace-up boots in black, brown and tan.

6. Dark Bottom, Colored Top

As I mentioned in chapter 3, I came up with a fairly simple solution for myself: Pear-shaped, like most women, I feel most comfortable and look best in dark slacks or skirt and tights. But because head-to-toe black is too boring and severe for me, I add my neutral-toned jackets and sweaters, often with a white blouse under them. If your upper half is your better half, I add this suggestion of Eleanor Lambert, creator of the International Best-Dressed List: "Save interesting details and colors for above the waist—people will notice your face first, not your hips."

The unifying principle behind each of these strategies is what we call THE RULE OF ONE. One color, one palette, one silhouette, one outfit . . . ONE STYLE!

The single idea that rings through all these approaches is that simplicity and discipline are necessities. Very few women have the time, interest, money, talent and lifestyle to support a wardrobe that requires Imelda Marcos's closetful of shoes and a dedicated ladies' maid. Yet you may feel these suggestions threaten you. Examine your resistance. Where's the variety? you may wonder. Where's the excitement? Where's the unexpected? Not to mention, what will you do with all that extra junk hanging in your closet now?

If your do feel threatened ask yourself: Is this what I want from my *clothes*—excitement, variety, thrills? Sadly, we've observed that for many women what they really want in their *lives* appears only in their *closet*. My friend Lisa kept buying little cocktail dresses whenever she shopped. One day, she had what we call a moment of fashion enlightenment. "I never *go* to cocktail parties," she confessed. "But I can't stop buying these dresses. I think I want to live the life I'm shopping for." There *can* be fun, pleasure, and excitement in *your* closet, but it should be based on your reality. If you don't have a place to wear a dress you want to own, then change your life, not your wardrobe.

A few other rules to remember as you "try on" a style.

Accept that you can't *be* everything. Letting go is a part of this process.

Accept that you can't *have* everything. Even if you could afford to, it wouldn't help you to look better. And, in the words of comedian Steven Wright, if you did have everything, where would you put it?

Pick the things you can live in most comfortably and happily. Some things look good but don't feel good. Others are the reverse. People tell me that I look good in red, and I can see that I do. But I don't feel comfortable in red. So I've given it up. Decide on the things that work best both ways. We all want to find the utopian place where comfort meets good looks.

GETTING HELP

or

Finding a Fashion Guru

> "When the student is ready, the Master appears."
> —Chinese proverb

Warning: Do not read this chapter until you have completed 1 through 6! And, if you have already found yourself in your closet, skip this chapter altogether. But, if you are more confused and disheartened than before, this chapter may provide relief. Do not read while driving or operating heavy machinery. Do not mix this chapter with alcohol and do not read it while pregnant.

So, you went into your closet to find yourself and there was nobody home. Or, worse, it seemed like a crowded costume party that you weren't invited to. Or (horror!), you realized that you hated yourself and that your clothes advertised it.

What to do? There's only a limited amount of direction that any guidebook can give. At a certain point, when lost in the back alleys of Katmandu, you need to give up on the map and ask for help. To quote a friend's favorite Spanish proverb: Ask and you shall find Rome. (Or maybe Paris, or Cincinnati, depending on how you want to dress!)

If at this point you still *don't* know how you want to dress, please do not feel as if you have failed, or that this book has failed you. Look at it this way: You have already gotten more in the way of enlightenment than you had bargained for. No wonder you never felt good in your clothes! There is no shame at this point in getting the help of a good mentor. Style is not about copying, it's about evolving, but we do often need help to evolve. When Eleanor Lambert was asked for her most basic advice on style she said, "Keep trying." As the beat writer Lew Welch put it, "Somebody showed it to me and I found it by myself." You still get full credit.

The trick, however, is getting the *right* help. Look for what we call the "Recognition Phenomenon": Just as you may have met or read about someone able to articulate perfectly the thoughts that you have trouble expressing, so there may be someone who can point you toward the perfect clothing that you have unknowingly been seeking. This process should not involve a slavish submission to anyone. (Remember, *I* learned from Amy's example, but I *never* copied her style.) Rather, it's a revelation of self—not unlike good psychotherapy.

This chapter outlines the six means of getting fashion assistance.

- **Finding a friend to help**

- **Finding a saleswoman you can trust**

- **Finding a stylist**

- **Finding a personal shopper**

- **Finding a boutique that carries clothing you like**

93

• Finding a woman whose style you admire

Each can deliver up style enlightenment, but be aware that each is fraught with perils. If you've been through the steps already outlined and still need fashion help, try one (or more) of these alternatives:

FINDING A FRIEND TO HELP

Now, do we have to define "friend" for you? We *aren't* talking about someone who's jealous, someone with whom you compete, someone who seems to sabotage your efforts at love, diets, professional success— even though she may purport to be your buddy. And don't do this with a blood relative. (*Especially* a sister— so much emotional baggage, there'll be no strength left to carry shopping bags!) So who *should* it be? A woman whose opinion you respect, a woman who dresses well, someone whose style you admire. It is not necessary that she be physically similar to you—Amy is nearly my opposite—but it might help. What's important is that she have your best interest at heart, your trust, a generous spirit and a good eye. A flair or gift for fashion is a great asset, and many women would be complimented to be sought after for advice.

Once you've chosen someone, here are some guidelines that you might want to keep in mind:

Suggest that your first foray be only exploratory— explain that you want to look and try on *but not buy.*

This takes the pressure off both of you. In our experience women buy together but they return alone. (Did you feel that chill wind?) Don't get overcome by your friend's thrill in the moment, or swept up into her enthusiasm for spending *your* money.

The acid test is returning by yourself to the shop, trying on selections calmly, and seeing if, in fact, you've struck gold. (By the way, many retailers will hold your choices without even a deposit if they smell an upcoming sale.) But you may not have a friend with the time, taste or temperament to help. Which brings us to the next option.

FINDING A SALESWOMAN YOU CAN TRUST

Remember: Smiles, compliments and coaxing words are not necessarily to be heeded from a saleswoman who will be making a juicy commission from your purchases. Any *good* saleswoman knows that a passionate but regrettable one-purchase-stand is worth less to her than a stable, long-term relationship. But most saleswomen *aren't* good. Also, bear in mind that while many saleswomen are motivated strictly by finances, there are those few professionals who are in the business because they love beautiful clothes. These traits are not mutually exclusive. Use several criteria to judge the real value of a salesclerk. Ask yourself these questions.

- Does she exclaim "This is you!" even though she's never laid eyes on you before? (And are you looking behind you to see if there's someone else for whom she's holding up that yellow fake monkey-fur jacket?)

- Is she dressed in a way that you admire or want to emulate?

- Is she helpful rather than pushy?

- Does she seem condescending and snooty or excessively complimentary and fawning?

- Did she at first ignore you when you wanted help?

- Does she guide you to an outfit that you feel wonderful in or does she put you in something that paralyzes you with doubt?

- Even though you set a dollar range, does she steer you to much more costly items?

Once again, the safeguard here is time. *Don't buy anything.* A useful, knowledgeable vendor can be a great help in formulating a wardrobe but, like any good relationship, it won't develop overnight. Come back and try on her selections later, preferably without her. Only then should you consider purchasing them. And, whatever you decide, try not to worry about what *she* thinks about you.

I have had great help from some sales staff. At one department store, I know a saleswoman who even calls to tell me when items I like are going on sale. Kate, of Saks Fifth Avenue in Bal Harbour, once awarded me a credit when items I bought were significantly reduced in a sale right after I purchased them. Nice help, if you can get it.

FINDING A STYLIST

A fashion stylist works for magazines, catalogues and advertisers, creating the look and mood of a model. The secret weapons of makeup artists, hairdressers, editors, designers and photographers, stylists are the unsung heroes and heroines of the fashion business. But they are certainly not unpaid.

Stylists don't usually work for the fashion consumer, but you may get lucky, for a price. How to find a stylist? Call an advertising agency in your town. Call or write a department store and inquire about an ad or catalogue picture they ran that you liked. Did they use a stylist? Who? Write to a magazine (numbers and addresses are listed on the masthead) and find out the name of the stylist responsible for a spread you are especially attracted to. (But remember, there is always a difference between what works in a photograph and what looks good in real life.)

FINDING A PERSONAL SHOPPER

This is a sort of combination of the two previous steps. Most better department stores now employ personal shoppers who can help with everything from a single special Christmas gift to entire wardrobes. This service is usually free of charge. Unfortunately, you do not always get to select the shopper. Often he or she is assigned, and although you may request a change, you don't get to audition everybody. Personal shoppers are usually (but not always) paid on salary, not commission. It is not impolite to ask which way they are compensated. If you find one who can efficiently take you from department to department, who can help match shoes to pantyhose and who respects and enhances your idea of yourself, then you may have found a guiding light on your quest for style. (And a tip may be appropriate if her service is extremely helpful.)

FINDING A BOUTIQUE THAT CARRIES CLOTHING YOU LIKE

My friend Diana, who lives in Washington, found a shop across from her office where almost everything suits her. Not surprisingly, the boutique owner is built a lot like Diana and has her very dark, dramatic coloring. Diana has been shopping there for three years now, and says, "Eighty percent of my wardrobe comes from that boutique."

We're not all this lucky. Finding a shop where the styles, the price tags and the variety are in line with your needs is not easy, but often a small boutique is less confusing and more service-oriented than a retail giant. First of all, the editing of every season's offerings has already been done by the buyer. And your requests and inquiries will be acted upon. Boutiques will often special order for you and provide or recommend the best place for alterations.

Finally, if all else fails, there is the strategy of imitation.

FINDING A WOMAN WHOSE STYLE YOU ADMIRE

If you really are having trouble identifying how you'd like to look, and who you'd like to be, think of someone, dead or alive, famous or obscure, whose style and personality you admire. She doesn't even have to be someone you know. In fact, Christian Louboutin believes you should "never try to look like your best friend or your daughter." It could be Audrey Hepburn, Grace Kelly, Janis Joplin, Roseanne, Diana Ross, Cindy Crawford, Cher, your favorite aunt or your fiercest competitor at work. (Amy says that Barbie was her major influence.) Watch her, learn from her, mimic her (but don't let her know what you're up to; she may be more irritated than flattered). Also, it helps to choose a style role model who is the same general physical type as yourself. And remember, this is meant to be a stopgap technique, not a permanent solution. But as *Homo sapiens* we do learn by emulation. Imitate a style until you feel comfortable and you make it your own.

Q&A Designer

Q: What celebrity personifies style to you?

A: Not only one, thank heavens: I can mention
Princess Caroline of Monaco for her innate class
accompanied by marvelous simplicity. I can mention Michelle Pfeiffer for her fantastic modern,
unadorned beauty or Omella Muti, together with
Maria Grazia Cucinotta as the style symbols of the
Mediterranean women . . . How many more? Certainly more than one.
              —*Giorgio Armani*

A: Audrey Hepburn. Elegance.
              —*Mary McFadden*

A: Susan Sarandon. She's at once sexy, cozy, sub-
lime, funny.
              —*Todd Oldham*

A: Mrs. Pamela Harriman. Certainly of a certain age, but always perfectly turned out and appropriately dressed for her role in public and private.
—*Bill Blass*

A: Gala Dali, Louise Nevelson, Lou Andréa Salomé, Alma Malher, Lee Miller.
—*Sonia Rykiel*

A: Louise Nevelson, Diana Vreeland, Ava Gardner, Jodie Foster, and Joan Crawford.
—*Emanuel Ungaro*

A: Marlene Dietrich for her liberty and invention and the Maharani Gayatra Devi.
—*Christian Louboutin*

A: Orlando—who gets the best of both worlds.
—*Fernando Sanchez*

DRESS REHEARSAL

or

I Thought I Liked It When I Put It On

> "In the beginner's mind there are many possiblities, but in the expert's mind there are few."
> —D. T. Suzuki

Okay. By now, from your closet or with a little additional help, you have managed to put together what we call a core wardrobe. Based on your meditations, your self-assessment and your fearless expedition into your closet, you've come up with an edited wardrobe of your favorite and most becoming pieces. So now it's time for a trial run because you may find, as I did, that a few of your selections still don't work.

What you need to look at now are the real-life wearability factors. We've broken them down into five general categories:

- **Comfort (Again!)**

- **Cleanability**

- **Practicality**

- **Appropriateness**

- **Fit**

To make this last assessment easier for you, we have created an evaluation card that allows you to rate these factors for any one of your outfits quickly. We use the old "one-to-ten" scale, with one being as uncomfortable as a Queen Elizabeth I costume (complete with neck ruff and wig) and ten being your old Dr. Denton's. We think anything that comes in with a rating of five or below ought to be reassessed and—unless you love it more than life itself—perhaps put aside.

How to use this evaluation form: Make a few photocopies and label each one at the top with the outfit you will be wearing. At least two times during the day (before lunch and when you take it off are good for us) assess how you feel in your outfit. Now average them. Anything that scores under a five on average, or that scores less than a three in any single category, should probably be eliminated from your wardrobe.

SIMPLE ISN'T EASY
EVALUATION CARD

OUTFIT

CATEGORY	RATING 1–10			
Comfort	AM	PM		RETAIN
Cleanability	AM	PM		◯
Practicality	AM	PM		REJECT
Appropriateness	AM	PM		◯
Fit	AM	PM		

Comfort

Amy defines an outfit as "comfortable" when she can put it on and "not ever have to think about it again until I take it off." It's a definition that works for me. For instance, Amy has two fabulous bracelets that she often wears in the summer. Each one consists of what looks like a thousand tiny seashells. The noise and the weight of them around my wrists would drive me nuts. And I'm not alone on this. Designer Mary McFadden, above all things, "detests charm bracelets on a woman." But Amy loves them and never gives them anything but an admiring thought. My friend Diana can't bear to wear anything made of wool against her hypersensitive skin, but I find wool not just comfortable but cozy. Because comfort (as pointed out in chapter 5) is in the psyche of the wearer, and not in the garment or a rule written in this book, we recommend that you "road test" each of your selected outfits to ensure that *you* feel really good in them.

Cleanability

You don't have to have a doctorate in Environmental Science to know that the world is not a kind place for white silk. If you have reduced your wardrobe to a lean closet, you will be crippled, impoverished and left naked if your clothes are not available to you because they are constantly at the cleaner's. Many factors affect a garment's ease of upkeep and cleanability. Whites, creams and pastels more obviously show dirt, while dark colors attract lint. Synthetics retain stains, but white silk will yellow over time (and not just under the arms). If a garment spends more time at the cleaner's or in the hamper than in your closet, it simply might not be workable. And, in this category, we also mention for your consideration the wrinkle-resistance factor. Some fabrics crease like an accordion the moment they are put on. Aside from natural linen, most don't look good wrinkled. My editorial assistant, Nancy, read the draft of this book, decided on a look and went out and bought four white cotton shirts—her favorite. But she found they spend too much time waiting to be washed and ironed. She's back to knits.

Practicality

Do these clothes function as they are meant to? If they have pockets (my clothes *must*) are they too high or too low for your hands? If there is a front vent do you need to keep your legs wrapped around each other like a garbage bag's twist tie in order not to show your crotch? (This is assuming you're not into Sharon Stone flashing.) The neck may be flatteringly high and stiff, but are you breathing? And while the waist is attractively nipped do you end up feeling like the girl in the magician's act, sawed in half? When you bend over to pick up your pet cat does the seam covering your butt scream for mercy? Your clothes should move with you, not against you, as you conduct the ordinary business of your life. They can be fussy or plain, but as long as they have the practical function of covering you where you want to be covered and giving you mobility when you want to move, they should stay in your wardrobe. If not, be ruthless.

Appropriateness

As we pointed out in chapter 1, what's fine for a cocktail waitress in a pick-up bar may not do for teaching a classroom of seventh grade boys (though *they* might not object). You may love that lush, full-length mink that cost you a bundle but—animal rights aside—wearing it to your job as a social worker may just alienate a few clients, not to mention your boss. Something you have may be appropriate for certain aspects of your life but not others. You may want to reserve a few dresses too dowdy for your job or your social life to wear to dinner at your in-laws' or to visit your niece's convent grammar school.

Clothes don't make the woman, but they can unmake her at the job. I know a woman whose work is exemplary; she held a position as executive director of a major nonprofit foundation. When her annual appraisal was done, she received performance ratings of "excellent" from all of the board members, but they did comment that her schleppy Sixties wardrobe "lacked professionalism." It affected her raise. She was, above all else, surprised. She had no idea anyone noticed. So, when we discuss appropriateness it is not only *your* own opinion that counts; it is also the approval in the eye of the beholder. You must be sensitive to the effect you create and the way you are perceived by those around you. Then, if you decide to disregard opinion, as she did, know the cost.

Fit

Amy's favorite old Hollywood publicity photograph shows a studio costume department's collection of dress forms, each a different shape and size, and each labeled with a different star's name. On most of these figures, padding had been added here and there to reflect the changing contours of the leading ladies' bodies. Whatever their weight, once dressed, those old-time stars' figures always looked alluring, thanks to the ingenious fits provided by clever costumers.

If you analyze a stylish woman—whether in a great old black-and-white movie or real life—you will notice something even more subtle than the quality of her clothes and the ease with which she wears them. One of the crucial reasons that she seems to be so "comfortable in her skin," as the French say, is that *her clothes really fit well.* I've often wondered how women who spend double-digit thousands on French couture clothes can possibly justify the expense (apart from the fact that the cost represents such a tiny fraction of their billion-dollar bank accounts). Well, I've spoken with some and these best-dressed women will not hesitate to tell anyone who cares to listen that there is nothing like having a jacket or gown fitted on them, custom-made to their own measurements. Standardized sizes fit nobody, except maybe some pattern-maker's dummy dress form.

You're no dummy. Sizes are just an estimate. They represent no physical, bodily reality, certainly not yours. So we recommend wholeheartedly that everything you buy or own, unless it is one of those stretch knit jobs that adapts to the wearer's shape, should be altered to your own individual dimensions by yourself, your friends or a professional. Many shops and department stores employ seamstresses to make these alterations (sometimes—but not often enough—free of charge). They can also refer you to a competent seamstress, if none is available on the premises. Dry-cleaners also usually offer a tailor or seamstress service. It's expensive but worth it. *One outfit that fits well is better than three that fit badly.* (By the way, this does not mean that you can buy any old garment and have it changed to suit your figure exactly. Often sleeves cannot be lengthened, there is no seam allowance to let out or a waist is simply too high and cannot be dropped.)

A garment should fit reasonably well even before you take it to be altered.

Amy has too often had a garment that she thought she couldn't live without altered and re-altered, only to find that she never wore it because, try as she might to turn her sow's ear into a silk purse, that perfect fit eluded her. And I have never bought a jacket whose sleeves I didn't have to have shortened—or else look like I was wearing my grandpa's coat! (No wonder stretch fabrics have been such a boon to the ready-to-wear fashion industry—they eliminate so much of the problem of fit.)

What's Next?

Well, at last! After this trial run and your final evaluation, you ought to feel pretty comfortable with your selections. Remember back at the beginning of this little book we promised that you could actually *make* money in this process? Now is the time. Your financial rewards are going to come from three different sources, and you may get some spiritual benefits as well.

It is time to go back to the boxes and bags of rejects. Yes, Virginia, you finally have to let go. But with that nice wardrobe you are living in, it doesn't hurt too much, does it? Divide your rejected clothes into those that are good enough for resale shops (these are listed in your local yellow pages), those that could be sold in a garage sale or flea market, and those that can be given to thrift shops and charities and used as a tax deduction. You may be amazed at how much cash you can generate from the first two. I hesitantly brought in a few of the better designer clothes I'd rejected because they, alas, were far too small for me. Not only did the retail store snap them up, the store's manager begged me to sell her the old suitcase I had brought them in! As Linda, one of my Florida neighbors who ran a sale with me, put it on our homemade sign: "Our junk, your treasures." I thought she had a lot of nerve, but you should have seen the cars pulling over and the women grabbing at those cotton jerseys!

As far as tax deductibility goes, some people need it and some do not, but we *all* need to do good works. Remember that all charities are not created equal: Some will give you a much higher write-off than others, and some distribute garments directly to the needy while others sell them for profit and use the money in a less direct way, to benefit a hospital for example. Check it out. I sent three big boxes of clothing to Goodwill Industries, while Amy dispatched a convoy of trucks to the Metropolitan Museum of Art's Costume Institute. (That about sums up the difference in our taste, connections and budgets!)

So, you've done some good works and may even have netted a profit. This is the part you have been waiting for! You have a new fund of money. What should you do with it? How about going shopping?

Now, we are not giving you *carte blanche* to fill those dresser drawers all over again. If the point of all this was to keep you in the endless squirrel's cage of fashion, that's how you jump back on the carousel. *That's not the point!* Sure, I was tempted. There was a Go-Silk outfit on sale at their outlet store that had my name on it. And I had made a little over two hundred dollars by selling off my goods (or "bads" as Linda called them). But the Go-Silk outfit didn't "go" with anything else I had and it wasn't on my list of necessities. Maybe it's on yours. I tried it on—twice—but I walked away from it.

So, how *do* you shop from now on? Turn the page to see.

SHOPPING

or

A Dangerous Game

> "Those who want the fewest things
> are nearest to the Gods."
> —Socrates

We all have confessions to make: shopping confessions. The most expensive mistake I ever made was a lavender leather suit. Go ahead and laugh. I deserve it. But I cried over that suit. It was as soft as rose petals and had been marked down from an obscene price to ninety-nine dollars. I did not have the money, or a place to wear the suit, or the right coloring to make it work. But I was desperate that day and it was so exquisite and such an enormous bargain! Seventy-five percent off at Neiman Marcus's infamous "last call." The salesgirl told me it was great and she was right. It *was* great for her if she could sell it.

You know the rest. I got home. I felt the excitement ebb as the thrill of the hunt turned into buyer's remorse. I tried it on at home and realized I looked ridiculous. But I hoped I could fix that. If only I could find the right shoes, and maybe if I lost just a few pounds and changed my make-up. (Not to mention my height, my face and my lifestyle, as well as my attitude.) The lavender suit was never worn by me. I couldn't even find a girlfriend to *give* it to. The only use I ever made of it was to hang it in a character's closet in my novel, *The First Wives Club*.

Linda, the Florida girlfriend of mine who owned a clothing store for many years, knows almost everything about shopping. And yet she tells me that sometimes even she opens her closet to find that

Sybil, her multiple personality, has been secretly shopping behind her back. She believes we all have a Sybil inside us forcing us to buy clothes that just won't work. But I believe that Sybil can be reckoned with.

To avoid horrible mistakes, extra expenses, wasted time, and the ruination of all of the work that you have done to organize your closet and create a personal style, **shopping must be controlled.** Now, since Americans are trained to shop as a leisure activity, this is going against every instinct we've got and every belief that is holy. The garmentos will hate us for telling you this. Too bad. I don't say it's easy but I do say it is possible to break the compulsive shopping habit. And it is *impossible* to have and keep a style if you are constantly tempted by random merchandise, "bargains" and impulse buys.

If you are committed to your excellent new look and to maintaining it, here are seven shopping rules to live by:

Don't Shop When You're Miserable

Know What You Are Looking For

Keep a "Needs List"

Don't Shop With the Wrong People

Don't Shop Alone

Beware of Sales

Avoid Extremely Trendy Styles

Don't Be a Magpie

✓ Don't Shop When You're Miserable

In twelve-step programs like Alcoholics Anonymous, there is a well-known and often quoted acronym: HALT. It stands for "Hungry, Angry, Lonely and Tired." People are advised not to let themselves act out when they are feeling any of the four. Overshoppers should follow the same guidelines. Too many women shop to alter their feelings instead of facing them. Last time you went shopping and came home—loaded with bulging shopping bags but still unsatisfied—were you seeking something other than another pair of midnight blue stilettos? Maybe what you *really* needed was a massage or a pleasant sexual interlude with your partner of choice. Or maybe you were just feeling anxious and guilty because you still haven't returned your mother's telephone call. Or maybe you were angry over the unfair criticism you got at work. The point is, take the time to figure out what's ailing you before you binge. (And remember: clothes shopping ranks second after gambling as the most *expensive* mood-altering addiction.) You will never achieve a personal style if you are using shopping as a stop-gap for self-knowledge or therapy.

So, if you find that you *have* been using shopping that way, and you can't stop, consider real therapy, a twelve-step program, deeper reflection on what is missing from your life, spiritual counseling, taking up a new hobby or (at the very least) shopping for something other than clothes.

✓ Know What You Are Looking For

Random shopping invites random purchases. You know what I mean: a scarf you adore but that doesn't work with anything you own, a dress you have no shoes for and that no coat will fit over. This is how binges begin. Kara, another Florida friend, once bought a pair of aqua suede driving gloves (marked down to almost nothing!) and wound up condemned to buy a matching suit, handbag, pumps, etc.—purchases which led to the final splurge of a white mink coat lined in aqua silk. In the words of Dave Barry, *I am not making this up!* A white mink. And remember, Kara lives in *Florida*.

On the other hand, my publicist in London, the svelte Karen Duffy, is such a controlled shopper that she can find the one perfect garment in a dreary thrift shop or jumble sale. Nobody can put together an outfit the way she can, and she rarely loses her head, even when tempted.

How can you emulate that? When you let impulse buying take over, remind yourself you are being controlled by the evil garmentos, the stores, advertising, not to mention your own *angst*. If true personal style is self-expression through dress, then, like any artistic form, it is achieved by discipline, control and balance. So when there is a lack in your wardrobe—a fabulous little black shift that needs to be replaced, a need for a new pair of warm pants, or when there is a change in the weather that mandates a heavier (or lighter) coat, it is important for you to define that need *before* you seek to fulfill it. Smart models know this. As cover girl Veronica Webb said, "I never go into the shops without knowing what I'm looking for. Otherwise one could go mad."

As we see it, shopping should be done not as a sport but with a specific goal in mind. Goals we approve of as specific and legitimate include:

> ***Upgrading an item that is shoddy.*** Nothing replaces quality. A well-made garment cut from fine cloth does not look like a cheap one, and there is no way to fake good craftsmanship and superior materials. Follow the dictum of Amy's friend, Babs, a retired fashion editor who says, "Buy less, and buy the best." By "the best," we mean the best you can reasonably afford. Remember, if the choice is between ten cheap and nasty suits and four good ones, you're better off with the latter. Amy's friend Joanne, for her first well-paying job after graduating from Harvard Law School, spent all her graduation gift money on three Chanel suits *and nothing else.* She wore them over and over again. They looked great, and so did she.

> ***Adding a basic that is missing from your closet.*** When I went through the closet experience, I realized I was the victim of a strange phenomenon: I had twenty-five jackets and shirts that looked pretty good but virtually nothing to wear

on the bottom! No wonder my closet was full but I didn't have a thing to wear! This realization only came about because of the *Simple Isn't Easy* approach, but once I noticed the pattern I knew the reason for it. I *like* the upper half of my body and I enjoy shopping for it. I can't say the same about my hips and thighs. But, after my realization, I also knew why I had such a hard time putting myself together. I simply didn't have any whole outfits. I was justified in going out and buying several pairs of trousers and a dress-up skirt. And it was interesting that—given my new knowledge—I *still* found myself drawn to blouses, jackets and sweaters. I had to force myself to concentrate on the items that I *needed*, rather than the items I *wanted* to buy. So, shopping for a missing necessary item is always legitimate.

Replacing a proven piece. Amy practically lives in black turtleneck sweaters on winter week-ends, but none of the ones she owned ever seemed just right (the neck was too loose, the wool was too itchy or the sleeves were too short). So, last year, she finally got rid of the inadequate ones and replaced them with a single, perfect black cashmere turtleneck (which cost as much as all the others added together!). If *you* have a useful item in your wardrobe and you can afford to upgrade it, that's the way to spend your shopping dollar.

With a leaner, more frequently used wardrobe comes a new problem: pieces that you love will eventually wear out. Heartbreak! A girlfriend of ours voiced this complaint: "After I sorted through my stuff, I did find the things that looked great on me, but they were things I always postponed wearing because I didn't want to spoil them!" Are *you* a secret hoarder? Would you wear a rumpled old cardigan and "save" the attractive one "for good"? Don't do it! I know it's a hard habit to break. But remember this is no dress rehearsal. This is your life! And if that's not enough, remember the story of my grandmother: Whenever she was given a present she particularly liked, she put it away "for later." After her early death, her other grandchildren and I had to go through closets and drawers full of beautiful things Nana had "kept for later." We cried. (Hey, you, blot that teardrop—it's time to wear things out and move on.)

Accept, then, that with the *Simple Isn't Easy* approach all the clothes in your closet should eventually be good ones and they are there to be enjoyed and worn out—in both senses of the word! But we do have a tip for you: When we find things that we adore and that we know will continue to work for us, Amy and I stockpile them: I have more than a dozen pair of a matte olive green pantyhose that I wear with the same color boots. (I'll never find either again!) And Amy has two pair of patent leather, low-heeled "rain boots." They don't make them anymore, and she wishes she had a third pair. But, despite care and stockpiling, clothing *will* wear out.

That means that legitimate shopping for replacements of your navy woolen coat-dress or your black suit will happen. Just don't allow yourself to become distracted and replace the navy woolen coat-dress with a floor-length magenta satin formal! (Not unless you're planning to change your whole look and your whole life to become a torch singer!)

✓ Keep a "Needs List"

To rework a line from P. J. O'Rourke, going into a department store with a Gold Card and no objective is as dangerous a combination for a woman as car keys and a six-pack are for a teenage boy. So, after the closet clean-out, I began to keep a needs list: *things I was certain I needed and would wear.* At one time last season my needs list looked like this:

A black tropical-weight wool jacket (double breasted?)
Black silk slacks
Brown leather shoulder bag (to match brown coat)
Good-looking rubber boots (impossible to find!)

I found that it's helpful to have an idea of the style and color of a needed garment, but you may not be able to find exactly what you want and then the trade-offs begin. I also find it helpful to carry a swatch or some threads from the clothes in the main colors I try to match. (You can even tape them to the inside cover of this book.) **But what you must not do is buy stuff OFF your list.**

So what happens if you see a fabulous sweater in just the right color that would really be great with every pair of jeans and trousers that you own? *Plus*, it's marked down to half price. You're going to hate me for this, but I say forget about it. In your heart you know that three out of four times you bring it home and it *doesn't* match your trousers, or you add it to your pile of sweaters and only wear it once a year. The point is you already *have* a sweater or two or three (or a dozen if you haven't been following instructions) that does the job nicely. And if you don't, then the sweater ought to be on your "needs list" already. Right?

In case of absolute emergency, when you see something *so* perfect, *so* wonderful, such a good buy, such a life-changer that you feel you'll die without it . . . don't buy it. But you can put it on hold. It's a compromise. Insist on a cool-down period. Reread this book, sleep on it, go back and look at your spare but fabulous closet and ask yourself if you really *need* it. Then determine what you will give away if you *do* get the item.

If, after all of that, you buy the thing, Amy and I hope it works for you. We've done the best we can.

✓ Don't Shop Alone

This rule may be broken by certain people—Amy regularly shops alone. But no one should shop alone when bored, depressed, recently fired or newly estranged from a husband. (Or right after leaving a shrink's office.) It's like that old rule for grocery shopping: Don't shop when you're hungry.

While researching *Fashionably Late*, I noticed that the compulsive shoppers were those who showed up at the mall day after day and—like serious drinkers—they *always* shopped alone.

✓ Don't Shop With the Wrong People

We know this sounds like something your mother told you, but if she *did* tell you this, it was one of the few times she was right. I love my girlfriend Melody, but she's not a good influence when we're shopping. She's too kind to tell me I look lousy in something when I do and she wants an excuse to spend money so she pushes me to spend mine. Friends like Melody are best to visit museums with—museums that don't have gift shops!

And don't shop with one of those "friends" who tells you how bad you always look in pants, or "helps" you by suggesting a diet that worked for her. We've all been demoralized by fluorescent bulbs in scary clinical white dressing rooms. We don't need help from "friends" who habitually put us in an even more unflattering light!

There are also those who are loving friends but just don't have a sense of style. They don't even recognize style when they see it. As the Chinese poet, Lin-Chi, put it:

When you meet a master swordsman,
show him your sword.

When you meet a man who is not a poet,
do not show him your poem.

Beware of Sales

I interviewed a vice president of a major fashion department store who explained to me how most sales worked. "We will lower prices on some things," he said, "but the really good stuff usually sells before the sale at full price." By the end of the season—while you *can* get a great buy—there's often a reason why the stuff is so marked down.

Again, if you know that you need a navy coat and you have a pretty good idea of what it ought to look like, there's no reason not to wait until the traditional Columbus Day mark-downs. But, because you are no longer impulse buying, and because you now have a clearer idea and a more discerning judgment about what you want, you may realize that you can only get it at the beginning of the season when the selection is widest. And because you are buying less, the sales savings may be immaterial.

Avoid Extremely Trendy Styles

Todd Oldham revealed that the most comon mistake he sees women make is "wearing what someone else says is in." If you're buying just to jump on this season's bandwagon it's a mistake—unless the purchase is fairly disposable, like a tight-fitting T-shirt or leotard in this season's newest color. You may, on the other hand, adopt some trends which you *know* always work for you and turn them into your own classics, regardless of what's on the runways or in the magazines. Through the last drop in hemlines, both Amy and I continued to wear short skirts, secure in the knowledge that this was our favorite and most flattering hem length. Amy says, "Long skirts weigh me down and short skirts—because they free the legs—give me more mobility. Besides, on both men and women, legs are my favorite part of the body."

As a fashion writer, Amy is often asked by women outside the industry, "Will my (select one) corset bustier/bell-bottoms/platform shoes/big-shouldered jacket still be in style next year?" Amy's answer to such questions is, "If you feel you look good in it, and you love it, wear it. And if you don't, discard it."

✓ Don't Be a Magpie

A magpie zooms in indiscriminately on every shiny little gimcrack that catches its eye, then schleps the stuff back to its nest. Whether it's real gold or tinfoil, the magpie brings it back home. Amy and I want you—unlike the magpie—to be able to see past surfaces and into essences. This may take a little concentration, but it's not really different from being able to tell that one brand of fudge ripple ice cream has oozier chocolate veins than another. Don't be seduced by a cheaply made nightgown with dazzling gold lamé inserts, shiny bows and frou-frou lace trim while passing up a quieter, simpler—but beautifully bias cut—gown with less of what the garmentos call "hanger appeal."

As an exercise, look in a large department store and see if you can distinguish the differences between a lower-priced and a higher-priced handbag of similar design. Or the difference between a well-made, expensive belt and a knock-off of it. A fleeting glance will reveal only similarities, but if you linger to touch, smell (don't insert in nostrils!) and handle the weight of both belts, they may begin to vary considerably. If you are not buying hastily, in a giddy, altered state of mind, you're a lot less likely to be fooled by inferior, gimmicky merchandise which will only (like a handsome, but heartless boyfriend) disappoint you in the end. If you're thinking that you can't afford to buy the better version, and you have no choice but to get the imitation, remember one of our few rules: that you should buy the best but buy less. And maybe, if you can't get a really good one, you should pass up the purchase entirely.

ACCESSORIES
AFTER THE FACT

or

Finishing Touches

> "Deciding what to wear 'beyond the dress' is not easy, but it makes the difference between elegance and non-elegance."
> —Giorgio Armani

> "Everything should be made as simple as possible, and no simpler."
> —Albert Einstein

One of my favorite cartoons shows a fashionable woman, illustrated in the over-the-top style of True Romance comics, saying, "I'm so grateful for my God-given ability to accessorize."

Silly as she may seem, the knack of putting the right finishing touches on an outfit *is* a rare and enviable gift. As Giorgio Armani told us, "The wrong accessories are the most common mistakes women make." And accessory adeptness is *not* a question of matching the belt to the bag to the shoes to the nail polish. That approach is as hopeless as trying to create a masterpiece with a paint-by-numbers kit. Like good painting, accessory adeptness is about adding, eliminating, balancing, contrasting and arranging textures, colors, shapes and proportions. Armani gave us some examples of typical problems. "Bags which are out of proportion to one's body, heels which are too high on women that are too short, too much jewelry." Fernando Sanchez says, "The wrong accessories most destroy a woman's style." And they can make the difference between a ho-hum outfit and a knock-out.

If you feel you, too, have a "God-given ability" then, like some of the world's chicest women, you might want to go to accessory extremes and make an indelible style statement. In the Jazz Age, the eccentric shipping heiress Nancy Cunard startled her contemporaries with her ivory bracelets, stacked from wrist to elbow. She could have afforded diamonds, but ivory was more original (and not endangered back then). Oil heiress Millicent Rogers covered herself in overscale Native American turquoise and silver jewelry, some pieces of her own design. *Vogue* editor Anna Wintour is rarely without her signature dark glasses (and *never* without them at fashion shows) or the highest Manolo Blahnik heels.

If, like me, your accessorizing skills are more modest, or your job requires conservative dress, you are better off playing it down and adorning yourself with, at most, one or two trademark pieces. I habitually wear a sumptuous scarf draped across my shoulders. Amy totes a fabulous polka-dot Gene Meyer handbag almost everywhere she goes. Wendy Goodman, *Harper's Bazaar* style director, always wears a changing assortment of unusual charms—a crystal, a seal, a baroque pearl, a branch of coral—suspended from a long cord.

Although just about anything from a tiara to a paper bag can be considered part of your outfit, there are usually ten basics to consider:

Shoes

Handbags and Schlepbags

Jewelry

Scarves

Hats and Gloves

Sleepwear and Loungewear

Briefcases

Glasses

Hosiery

Coats

Shoes

Stilettos, spectators, pumps, slingbacks, platforms, clogs, boots! The sight, smell and feel of a new pair of shoes excites a stylish woman's senses more than a parure of jewelry or a pan of fresh brownies. No doubt about it, women are obsessed with shoes. They boast about the number they own, one-upping each other like old guys with their fish stories. For my money, shoes are the Number One Most Important Accessory. Mary McFadden agrees: She told us, "The single thing that destroys a woman's style are bad shoes." Like a rotten egg whipped into a souffle, badly made or poorly cared for shoes degrade the rest of your look, no matter how elegant or costly. And of all articles of clothing, shoes are probably the most accurate index of taste. Yves Durif, Amy's hairstylist, says he surreptitiously studies a new client's shoes as a way of gauging her character. In the old Studio 54 days, the doormen used to decide whom to turn away on the basis of their footgear! Although I abhorred Imelda Marcos's politics, I understood her shoe closet. Most women have an unlimited appetite for shoes.

No two pairs of feet are built alike, and even your own two feet are not identical. Yet sizes are standardized as if one 8B were the twin of every other (and wider and narrower widths are now rarer than unicorns—that's why women *develop* corns!). In the old, pre–mass production days, shoes were designed, as clothing was, on the body of the individual who wore them. Well, at least you can alter your dresses—but almost nothing can be done about shoes that don't fit. So let's get to it! *Simple Isn't Easy* techniques strike again! Toss out of your closet those shoes that were supposed to "give" or "stretch." They almost never do—or not enough anyway. (Shoemakers can sometimes stretch the width of a shoe, but *never* the length.) Amy says that when you request a stretch, make sure to ask for a "toe box" stretch too, to create as much extra space as possible. If you absolutely can't resist a marked-down pair of shoes in the wrong size, buy too large—*never* too small. You can insert insole cushions to reduce them somewhat.

As always, when a difficult question is raised, we find an answer in one of our hallowed *Simple Isn't Easy* precepts. **Find the shoe label that fits your foot best and stick with it. Be a shoe loyalist. The right shoes feel good from the start, without any breaking in period.**

Shoe mania can easily get out of control. (Look at Imelda.) Remember then that there is a definite disadvantage to having too many pairs. The difficulty is that both slacks and skirts will each have their own ideal shoe height and shape. A pair of slacks that look terrific with a chunky two inch heel will look lousy with a spindly one inch one. It can be a lot of extra trouble keeping track of which shoes go with which hem lengths. Amy solves this problem by having one pair of shoes designated for each of her dresses. (But then she *does* have two walk-in closets. She *claims* she reserves one pair of shoes for walking into her walk-in closet!) My way of keeping it simple is to have all of my slacks hemmed for two-and-a-half inch stacked heels. And I wear my skirts with three inch pumps. Another easy solution for pants that Amy proposes is to wear them with ankle-high boots. (Toned-in hosiery is then less of a problem . . . it's not visible.)

Finally, bear in mind this astute advice from Parisian shoe designer Christian Louboutin: "Shoes are not really about fashion. What matters is not whether high or low heels are 'in,' but that a woman walks and moves beautifully and gracefully in them."

Handbags and Schlepbags

Quality over quantity, as always, is the best *Simple Isn't Easy* principle for bags, too. Marcia Sherrill, the dynamic designer for Kleinberg Sherrill hand-bags, gives the following sound (and not necessarily self-interested) advice. "A bag should be an enduring thing," she says. "Buy some-thing tried and true, devoid of a lot of gim-micks, something that can see you through as many occasions as possible, and that you can wear absolutely every day. Stay away from suede and fabrics—they don't wear as well as leather. A good rule of thumb: a bag should cost about the same amount as what you would normally spend on one outfit. Don't scrimp! Bags are as telling as shoes."

It helps to define what bag works best for your needs, and your wardrobe. For day and evening I stick with a shoulder bag because I need to have my hands free. Coco Chanel designed the first shoulder strap bags to free women's arms, so this may be important to you, too. Amy prefers structured bags with a handle rather than a shoulder strap, because her clothes tend to have sharp, precise lines. She doesn't like shoulder straps because they mar the drape. Maria, a writer friend who has had a back problem, likes stylish backpacks because they give the arms more freedom—and they complement her sporty clothing. None of us has time to change our bag daily to match our changing outfits. (By the way, whatever style you pick, ruthlessly edit the contents of your bag so that it does not resemble a badly sorted recycle bin.)

Jewelry

We both agree that when it comes to jewelry, forego the puny little "genuine" pieces (tiny butterflies on a chain, microscopic diamond chips in a weeny heart suitable for a sweet sixteener). We've got not a thing against the real goods, mind you, just the namby-pamby non-sense that does nothing for anybody except the jewelry retailer. (An insider's secret: Those minuscule gold nothings have the highest markup of all and have virtually no resale value.) So, if you must have real gold, choose one gold something over lots of gold nothings—even if you have to wait to accumulate the cash for it. Or, instead, put your money on an important costume piece. I buy a lot of my stuff from Jaded—a New York costume shop. And I love pieces by Steven Vaubel. (Amy's friend, the costume jewelry designer Mish, says that his work "imitates nothing—it's genuine Mish!")

Overloaded and understated are both good looks. Just make sure you have the panache to pull off the former and the restrained elegance to carry off the latter. Chanel wore tons of necklaces—mixing faux with real in a revolutionary way. And Helena Rubinstein—*all* of her piled gems were the real thing, dear—mixed precious and semi-precious, colored stones (her passion), baroque pearls and diamonds. The fact that she was barely five feet tall did not stop her from thinking "the bigger the better!" Great, though maybe not for the laundromat or the average working girl!

The safest and easiest jewelry to wear is the brooch. A well-designed pin adds a touch of sparkle to a lapel or neckline without a lot of hassle. I wear a (fake) gold cameo-shaped pin almost daily. It's Medusa's head and as you know, she had the power to turn men to stone. I've needed that in business at times! It's my gold badge of courage.

As I mentioned, Amy often wears two bracelets—one on each wrist. They complement her long, muscular arms and tinkle and glisten in a seductive, subtle way. But Amy doesn't teach piano and isn't a court stenographer. If *you* are, be aware that bracelets can be noisy and distracting at business meetings or presentations.

Earrings are my private addiction. I'm always searching for the perfect pair. And they don't take up much room. But as a *Simple Isn't Easy* philosophy, don't let mistakes clutter up your jewelry box. Toss out, give away, sell or trim your Christmas tree with all the baubles in your drawer that you have not worn in the last millennium.

Scarves

For color, fantasy and drama, or neatly tailored chic, the scarf is the most versatile of all accessories. These basic rectangles or squares of cloth are the simplest unit of clothing, yet because they come to life only through the wearer's creativity, they are also the most intimidating. If you'd love the color and panache of scarves but can't get the knack of wearing them, I recommend taking a class to learn how to tie them. There are also instructional books available, though most overwhelm me with difficult diagrams and really weird knot suggestions. Pick just a few styles—and ignore the origami-like instruction on how to build a replica of the Eiffel Tower with your scarf. (Or ask a French acquaintance for help. They're all born with a scarf-tying gene, and they wear them as nonchalantly as their eyelashes.) Finally, whatever you do, don't tie that silken explosion of color into a boy-scout neckerchief. You're better off giving up on the whole scarf idea.

Hats and Gloves

Your great-grandmother only took them off for her bath, but when do *you* put them *on*? Hats can do more wonders for your face than the most deftly applied cosmetics, but how not to feel like a goon in one? Weddings, church and synagogue services—sadly, there are few, if any, other occasions that call for them anymore. For the women of the last century, and the first half of this one, hats had the same allure that shoes now hold for us. But Sixties bouffant hairdos, followed by the decade's relaxing of mores, brought about this dreadful hat obsolescence. All those lovely gestures and rituals, all those glorious possibilities for shape, color and trimming, all the intrigue and flirtation of the veil—gone, gone, gone! How sad! I'll never forget the eighteen months I lived in London. I got to wear hats all the time and there

141

no one thought it odd. (One small reason to keep the Royal Family going!)

If you're a hat fancier—if you've got a head for millinery—all is not lost. Amy is partial to headgear herself—neat, pillboxish affairs, or berets (never broad-brimmed picture hats or sweet country girl confections) and she has the nerve and style to wear them. But for the rest of us there are at least two (seasonal) excuses to keep hats on our heads, without looking inappropriate: Winter and Summer. One for warmth (you lose up to 80 percent of your body heat through your bare head) and the other for sun protection. But, whatever your excuse, *if you feel foolish in your hat, don't wear it.* It must be worn with security and confidence, even indifference. (This is how a stylish woman wears *all* her clothes.) I'll never forget the sun hat I bought in Martinique—expensive straw with a black grosgrain band. As I walked across the hotel patio to my chaise, a woman rushed up to me and breathlessly asked where I'd gotten the hat. I knew I had a hit. (And I told her I didn't remember!)

Sleepwear and Loungewear

There are some of us who look lovely by day and fall completely apart at night. Oh, I know *you* wouldn't do that, but just in case, I want to point out that it is very easy to create an attractive, around-the-house uniform. I have three pairs of white cotton pajamas for sleepwear and, over time, they have become soft and delightful. Meanwhile, I also have my beloved sweats—a collection of nice-looking and nice-fitting soft clothes that I wear at home.

My girlfriend, Linda, is a master at the creation of a comfortable at-home uniform. A stunning blonde, she admitted that she has spent over a thousand dollars on five of the exact same black DKNY muumuus that she slips on when she comes home from work. Just think: Her husband has never seen her in a ratty old robe. You may not be able to afford to spend the thousand dollars, but you don't have to. My pajamas were mail order, and I got my sweats at clearance sales. Amy adores Fernando Sanchez robes—especially those from his men's collection. And she also loves caftans for at-home wear, particularly when entertaining. Her favorite is a vintage Geoffrey Beene she found at a thrift shop!

Briefcases

Don't be one of the boys. Unless you're a female cross-dresser (and then you're reading the wrong book, honey) pass up the really masculine attaché case for a stylish, neat tote bag, oversized handbag, etc. Those hard-edged attachés belong in the same circle of fashion purgatory as that dated, female yuppie suit-with-sneakers look. And they hurt when they bump your leg.

Glasses

What do Sally Jessy Raphael and Sophia Loren have in common with *Vogue*'s Anna Wintour? Signature eyewear. Great eyeglasses or sunglasses are a fantastic look-maker, and a marvelous coverup on days when you are tired, or just couldn't deal with full eye makeup. If a frame works wonders on you, consider them as a cosmetic, no matter how much of a medical necessity they actually are. Have duplicates made in case the frames are discontinued, and if they are, search for an approximate replica.

Hosiery

The sheerest, smoothest, silkiest pantyhose always look the most graceful—and always cost more than supermarket brands, which tend to appear blotchy and grainy against the skin. So buy the best you can afford. All brands and all price levels of pantyhose snag, tear and run with maddening frequency.

Good-looking run-free hosiery is one of those commodities (like gasoline-free cars) for which the technology probably exists, but if it was introduced would kill off whole industries. Until durable sheer stockings see the light of day, here are some tips for stylish legs:

The greater the ratio of Lycra to nylon, the better-looking and the longer-lasting the hose.

Reinforced toes prolong the life of delicate stockings. But please don't wear with open or low-cut shoes because they compete with the design. (You already knew that, right?)

Flesh-colored stockings used to have a bad fashion rep, but good manufacturers make them now in tones that blend as beautifully into the skin as a good makeup base. They can make you legs look as smooth as a store mannequin's, and they're often prettier than ivory-colored stockings (which can get Alice-in-Wonderlandy). Plus you don't have to worry about matching legs to shoe or dress. And—should you get a run in the line of duty—it won't show as much.

Black opaque pantyhose, in either a shiny or matte finish, are very long lasting, and perennially stylish (they're a favorite of fashion folk). They're warm, slim-

ming, and superb with black suede shoes or boots.
Sheer black is also often an attractive choice.

When you find the pantyhose that function best for
you, buy stacks at a time and store them. And buy at
sales. Most stores run annual specials.

But if you think pantyhose were invented only for
bank robber's masks, then stay in slacks or long skirts.

Please throw out hosiery with pulls or snags, even if
there are no runs. They make your legs look diseased.
If you want to get more life out of them, wear them
under pants.

Garters and stockings do have the practical advantage of allowing one snagged leg to be replaced at a
time. But who can be bothered with the hardware? In
another lifetime I'll be the kind of girl who wears them.

Well, that about wraps up the accessory subject,
except for wraps themselves.

Coats

Coats are important for those of us
who live or travel to cold climates.
They are more than an accessory
since when you are wearing one it *is*
a total look. And in the winter, it is
what you are most seen in. But, all too

often, women seem to forget that the coat and what's under it ought to bear some relationship to each other. You know the disjointed look I mean—a frilly formal worn with a ski jacket. Well, perhaps I'm exaggerating, but you get the point.

Amy loves the idea of color in winter coats—so cheering on bleak days. For ten years she's worn the same long, lilac, shawl-collared swing coat in mohair—fantastic with black accessories. I keep to neutrals, but then for me *Simple Isn't Easy*. Some hints to help with coats:

- Be sure they slip easily over suit jackets, dresses, bulky sweaters.

- Beware of piling up shoulder pads on top of shoulder pads—you'll turn into a no-neck monster.

- Hems of skirts or dresses should not peek out below hems of coats, if it can be helped.

- At night and for parties, if you don't have a coat long enough to cover a full-length evening gown, wear a warm wrap or stole instead.

- The line of a beautiful coat will be destroyed if you sling your bag's shoulder strap over it diagonally, from shoulder to hip.

- Please save ski jackets for outdoorsy wear. Get a real tailored coat for city wear. Remember the rule of appropriateness.

You also won't be surprised to hear that I have a pair of gloves for each coat, which I stuff in the pockets, and a wool challis scarf for each one. The scarf is not only warm, it can cover a neckline where a blouse collar is popping out or a blazer makes an inconvenient bulge. The scarves also relieve some of the dullness of my purposely neutral coats. Whichever approach you choose, brights or neutrals, or whichever one you create for yourself, remember that the most carefully orchestrated look can be ruined by a coat that is only an afterthought.

Q: What do you detest on a woman?

A: Too much jewelry, too many accessories, too much makeup.

—*Bill Blass*

MAINTAINING THE
LEAN CLOSET

or

Keeping It Down

> "Darling, you don't need that.
> You have enough already."
> —Halston

When I was very young (and then not so young) I couldn't go to sleep at night unless the closet door was completely closed. It didn't matter how many times the light was turned on, the sliding door opened, the inoffensive contents revealed to me—I knew that powerful monsters lurked there. (Luckily, they weren't powerful enough to get out unless the door was left opened.)

Well, in a sense, even then I knew. As revealed earlier, most of us *do* have monstrosities hanging in our closets, and the condition of those closets themselves are pretty horrifying. You know what I mean: one garment flung over another; clothes swathed like Marley's Ghost in wretched and totally impenetrable dry-cleaner polyethylene; heaps of unidentifiable garments that have slid to the floor. Not to mention how you have broken Mommie Dearest/Joan Crawford's sacred rule: *no wire hangers ever!*

A well-organized closet is not just a comfort and a useful tool to a woman. It is a necessity. And it is also a reward for all of the work you have done. A closet's condition somehow corresponds with your mental state. How much more serene we feel when we know that behind closed doors all is clean, clear and orderly. Closet fantasies are intriguing: Amy has a recurrent dream that she opens her closet doors and, to her great delight, discovers within it extra space, wonderful new clothes, and organization. And whenever I feel overwhelmed, confused or bogged down, I straighten out my (already neat) closets.

Interestingly, designers and retailers have begun to understand and exploit the seduction of a beautifully organized closet. Just think of all of those closet makeover ads with before and after pictures! The closet rebuilding and organizing industry has developed virtually overnight into a booming seventy million dollar business. Donna Karan understood the lure of a well-coordinated closet when, one season, she actually asked Bergdorf Goodman to sell her clothes from a wardrobe. As an assistant explained: "Putting them in a closet is part of Donna's philosophy . . . the closet is a natural setting for the contemporary woman's lifestyle." For you to look good, your closet has got to look good.

This doesn't mean spending a fortune on built-ins or cedar paneling or wire basket holders. Because the greatest luxuries in any closet are not its fittings but its contents and space. And now, with your new, lean wardrobe, your closet should have all the space you need. But using the space well is an acquired skill, and I *did* get some tips from the experts. Just as artfully displayed clothing in a shop or boutique helps you to select and purchase it, beautifully displayed clothing in your own closet will help you to dress better each day. A small investment in closet fixtures will pay big dividends in savings. You'll have fewer repairs, no extra pressing charges and you won't be buying unnecessary garments simply because you can't see the ones you have! Brooke Stoddard, a very organized design assistant at *Harper's Bazaar*, has such a mania for visibility that she Polaroids each outfit and inserts the picture in a "style diary." She says, "I can leaf through my book instead of through my closet when I'm contemplating what to wear." Too much effort for most of us, but perhaps the idea may be a good one if you have the time, the interest and a fashion-related career.

To organize your lean closet, here is the basic list of closetware you may need to purchase:

Dress, Skirt and Slacks Hangers

Belt Holders

Shoe Storage Units

Purse Storage Shelves or Boxes

Scarf Hangers

Sweater Boxes

Hangers

I just about insist that any decent closet should be equipped with matching hangers. If you're wealthy and can afford scented, satin-upholstered, fabulous ones, fine. But I just use the standard clear plastic ones with metal hooks that swivel. I prefer these to the more modern one-piece white (or colored) plastic variety. Those require you to be careful which direction your clothing goes on them. It is important when hanging clothing in your closet to have everything face in one direction. This isn't just my neurotic compulsiveness cropping up. Visibility is the name of the game. And hangers of different heights and styles will make it difficult for you to compare the lengths and the cuts of the jackets and dresses arrayed before you. Since, in most discount stores, you can buy a set of a dozen hangers for a lot less than five dollars, there is no excuse for leaving things on the wire disasters that dry cleaners distribute. Those hangers also tend to damage the clothes by snagging them on the sharp end of their twisted wire, potentially leaving rust stains, as well as deforming the shoulder line of delicate or knitted garments. Why pay for expensive pressing only to find the blouse hanging crookedly with creases mashed in?

Now that you no longer have your communion dress, girl scout uniform, your old maternity tops, and the blazer from your first job all squashed into the closet, it shouldn't take long to take your final selection of clothing and arrange it on identical hangers, face forward. This exercise will also help you to clarify just one more time what you have in abundance and what, if anything, you may be missing.

There are several different approaches to arranging the clothes in your closet. As I mentioned earlier, I believe it is easiest to hang an entire outfit on a single hanger. For me, this includes the pants, the blouse and the jacket or blazer that I usually wear together. I go so far as to hang the scarf I wear with it on the hanger as well. For me, this arrangement works. I rarely substitute one piece for another, with one major exception—at the side of my closet I hang a couple of pairs of black slacks and a couple of skirts which I can substitute for any of the other bottoms in my collection. This really works well for me.

My sister, on the other hand, is a bit more obsessive-compulsive. She hangs all of her jackets together, then has a section of blouses, followed by one of skirts and trousers. The advantage to this system is that you can see everything you own a bit more readily. The disadvantage is that you actually have to remember which items goes with which.

Amy, who wears dresses or suits almost exclusively, uses a different but equally successful organizational method: She has all of her dresses and suits lined up by color, season and silhouette. Her closet is really beautiful to look into.

And that's part of the point here. We are working together to try to make dressing both a pleasant and easy part of your day. Opening a closet door to a snake-pit shambles and rooting through it only to find that the skirt you need for the jacket you selected is at the cleaner's, or that you simply cannot find the beige blouse you *know* has to be there, adds a nasty extra pressure to your already busy morning. When my closet is organized, I take pleasure in getting dressed, and when it isn't, I dress hurriedly, haphazardly and I end up unhappy with the results.

Belt Holders

If you are going to wear belts, you have to find a way to display them to select them as needed. There are all kinds of little gadgets in the marketplace: racks that can be attached to the back of a closet door, special hangers with belt holders attached, etc. Because I like to keep it simple (and because I don't have a lovely tiny waist) I only have two belts—a very expensive black leather one, which I wear most often, and a brown one. I keep these on a hook right at the front of the closet. But there are some other cloth belts that came with slacks or dresses. I simply keep these on the hanger with the garment they match. Whatever method you choose, the important principle is **everything must be visible** or else you'll forget what you own.

Shoe Storage Units

As I mentioned earlier, just about every woman I know has a streak of Imelda Marcos in her. But who can afford to house three thousand pairs of shoes? I tried at first to store my pared-down pairs in the plastic hanging shoe bags sold by department stores and mail-order catalogs. They didn't work for me. I couldn't see the shoes and it was a pain in the neck to have to unzip the long plastic "door" to get to them. Plus it took up a lot of valuable closet hanging space. After trying to keep them lined up on the closet floor (and invariably winding up with a dusty mess), I bit the bullet and got shoe racks. Each pair is now displayed neatly in its own compartment and I only have room for four-teen pairs of shoes (but that's not counting sneakers). I don't know if that's a lot or a little, but they are very good shoes!

Find what works for you. But *don't* keep shoes closed up in the cardboard boxes they came in. Our editor does this and says he likes to. But I believe you *will* for-get what you have and nothing wastes more time when you're running late than digging through closed boxes like a maddened ferret hunting for those green suede pumps you were *sure* you had in the front.

Purse Storage Shelves or Boxes

Most closets have what carpenters call "hat shelves" (though I don't know of anyone besides Amy who puts hats there). These are the shelves immediately above the closet pole. I find them a perfect place to keep my purses. This way, at a quick glance, I can see which one I need to wear on a given day or evening. *Don't* keep them wrapped up in the bottom of a drawer. This is another way to forget what you have and end up buying more of something you already own.

Scarf Hangers

Did I mention that I *love* scarves?! Since I tend to wear neutral-toned, fairly tailored clothing, I depend on scarves to give some movement and flow, some softness and femininity. And perhaps because of that I am more likely to be extravagant when it comes to buying a beautiful scarf than with any other purchase. (Since I wear them so often I feel the cost is justified.) But it has taken me a long time to find an efficient way to store them. I once read that Princess Grace stored her costly Hermés and Gucci scarves and shawls on slacks hangers, covering them first with acid-free tissue. Well, that's fine if you have the royal closet space, the time, the patience or the staff, but I don't. My sister had special cabinets built that let her fold hers away in flat, shallow drawers but most of us don't have the money for that kind of effort, either. And I believe that folding scarves and hiding them in drawers makes it more difficult to remember what you have and how you wear them. My solution, as I mentioned earlier, is to drape them over the hanger holding the outfit I wear them with. Amy's solution is equally viable: She gently rolls them in clear plastic stackable drawers so they are visible and easily accessible. An artist friend of mine in New York's SoHo hangs her scarves and her necklaces on pegs all across her vast loft wall, where they make a wonderful display of color and pattern (although I would worry about dust and dirt settling on them).

Sweater Boxes

As I've also mentioned, I love sweaters, but storing them has been the bane of my closets. If I fold them neatly and put them in dresser drawers I forget what I have and if I hang them beside my blouses, they stretch and lose their shape. The only answer that works for me are the transparent plastic (yes, we hate plastic) sweater boxes that I stack on the hat shelf of my closet. The benefit of using these is that it is easy to protect sweaters from moths and dirt. Amy keeps her sweaters in cubbyholes (which she originally had constructed for filing her papers!). If anyone has a better solution, do let us know.

And when you're tempted to buy more stuff, remember: **The most luxurious thing in your closet is SPACE.**

GROOMING AND
MAINTENANCE

or

Care and Breeding

> "She wears her clothes as if they were thrown on her with a pitchfork."
> —Jonathan Swift

Now that you have the beautiful clothes and the beautifully organized closet, you aren't done. Just as a gorgeous painting can be ruined through mishandling, so can the portrait of yourself that you have so masterfully created be spoiled if care isn't taken with these five basic points.

Wardrobe Maintenance

Haircare

Nail and Hand Grooming

Skin Care and Makeup

Scents

Because most of us have a life other than our closets and our looks, *Simple Isn't Easy* here takes a deeply practical view: To keep maintenance high, but not too time-consuming, we almost always vote for the simple approach. And Bill Blass, whose clients can spend unlimited amounts on maintenance, told us that what he adored on women was "simplicity in clothes, hair and makeup."

Wardrobe

Like a purebred show dog with a mangy coat, a superb wardrobe will appear degraded if buttons are missing, linings are unraveling, collars are dingy and sweaters are pilled. While superior quality clothes will wear better and last longer, they, like an expensive foreign car or a Cartier watch, require periodic tune-ups and proper maintenance. No less than its poor acrylic cousin, the most luxurious cashmere pullover can be spattered with tomato sauce, snagged on a prickly wicker chair or frayed at the cuffs by regular wear.

Diana Vreeland, whose bandbox fresh, immaculate elegance continues to be an inspiration to everyone who knew her, said that the most heavenly scent on earth was the smell of saddle soap on clean leather. She made a religion of grooming, loving all the implements and artisans associated with wardrobe maintenance, as well as the effects they produced. (Her maid actually polished the *soles* of her shoes, cleaned out the inside of her handbag and laundered and pressed her dollar bills.) Vreeland once even went so far as to say that she could live anywhere as long as there was a good shoe repairman in town!

Well, few of us have Vreeland's means, or this level of fanaticism, nor do our jobs depend on our personal style as hers did. But we can still profit from her example. Cleanliness is not only next to godliness, it's also the most fundamental component of style. (Unless, of course, you're in some Pacific Northwest garage band.) Nothing can undermine all the good style work you've done as completely as a grease stain on your lapel or a run in your hose (and no nail-polish touch-ups, please!).

The good news is that with fewer clothes, constant, vigilant stock-taking of your clothes' condition is not so onerous. With the contents of your closet streamlined, the hazards of mashed-in wrinkles, gaping seams or silk dresses slipping off hangers to the closet floor are diminished. But care is still of the essence, and it's easiest to keep up with maintenance yourself, when possible. The basic tools to ensure upkeep must be kept on hand. They include:

A Good Quality Steam Iron

Keep a supply of the requisite accessories—a can of spray starch, an ironing board (tabletop models will do if space is limited), distilled water, etc. Pressing is definitely a minor art, and the price you pay for dry cleaning is 25 percent cleaning and 75 percent pressing labor, because ironing takes patience and skill. Although some of us find ironing a relaxing, satisfying activity, others are past masters of the slow burn and sizzle. If ironing seems nothing more than a burdensome chore, if fabrics are too delicate or you're always in a hurry, consider purchasing the alternative:

A Professional Steamer

Yes, you know the kind we mean—the large bulky models you see in boutiques, or, alternatively, the hand-held, travel-size version. Amy thought long and hard before buying one of those upright steamers—it wasn't cheap and it was space-consuming. But, as ironing is about as appealing to her as grave-digging, she has never regretted the purchase. And she's saved a fortune in dry cleaning and pressing charges (while her iron now languishes in the back of a kitchen cabinet). Amy's sister, Erika, who has no room for such a full-size industrial tool, instead wields her travel steamer like a magic wand. And I know a flight attendant with a great stall shower—she hangs clothes from a hook she installed in her bathroom ceiling and lets the rising steam do the rest!

If you are really a slouch when it comes to banishing wrinkles, there is a canned, spray-on chemical product that does the trick. (Amy once heard a woman in the hardware store asking if the formula worked on faces too!) While none of the gizmos in this category will press a razor-sharp crease into your trousers, if you hate ironing, maybe you should consider that problem next time you want to buy a pair of finely tailored slacks.

A Sweater Shaver (or a regular electric shaver)

Even if you like your man with a little stubble, the attraction doesn't apply when it comes to your sweaters. Some knits seem to sprout fuzz faster than your underarms. Banish that two-day growth with a sweater shaver, which operates just like an electric razor. (We don't recommend waxing or any form of cream depilatory!) But be careful—shaving too often or too deep can nick the delicate fibers just as a razor can nick your skin. Except sweaters don't grow back!

A Lint Brush

A hairbrush-shaped tool, it dutifully collects all that flotsam and jetsam that people like to pick off your clothes when they're in an intimate mood.

A Tape Roller

Slightly more primitive than the above, but sometimes more effective. I keep one in the hall closet, one in my desk drawer, one in my suitcase and one in the bathroom. But then, I have both a cat *and* a dog, along with a preference for dark colors that attract everything but men and money. In a pinch you can practice the sticky-fingers technique and wrap masking or scotch tape around your pretty hands—sticky side out—and go to work. (One executive we know swears by self-stick mailing labels.)

A Small Sewing Kit

Even if it's just for an emergency, like stitching up a torn hem or securing a button that's about to take its death plunge, you need the basics—straight pins, needles and threads in a few colors. If sewing's not one of the domestic arts you've mastered, at least keep handy assorted safety pins for stopgap mending until you find an obliging friend or professional seamstress. And we don't have to tell you not to wait too long—or that a stitch in time is a good idea.

A Button Box

Most clothes come with an extra button or two, or even a bit of matching thread. Don't throw these out or stuff them someplace where they'll be forgotten or lost. Toss them into one large, covered container. My sister taught me the value of a button box, and I now have a pretty ceramic one sitting on my bedroom bureau.

A Suede Brush, Suede Spray and Spray Waterproofer

Don't let rain, mud, snow or sleet ruin your beautiful shoes and boots, even if they ruin your day. *Always* have a pair of what we call "rain shoes"—shoes that can take the weather—in patent leather or rubber to spare your most precious footwear from the elements. They don't have to look like duck's feet either.

Search them out—they are not only a lifesaver but a shoe-saver.

Because a well-made pair of shoes, well-tended, can have a very long life, be sure to weather-proof *all* your shoes before you wear them, though it may alter the color slightly. The healthier a patient is to start with, the better she mends. As we reminded you earlier, the better the quality of your shoes, the more responsive they are to good care.

A Tin or Tube of Neutral Leather Cream

You don't need a big shoe polish box and a host of different colors. Just a little soft rag, one tin of neutral polish and a lot of elbow grease—for purses and belts as well as shoes.

Spot Remover

A must for on-the-spot stain removal. Every couture workroom has stashes of them. As designer Gene Meyer says, "Full dry-cleaning can remove spots, but also take the life out of clothes." One that I like is called "White Wizard." It is a semi-solid and, when rubbed on a spot with a clean soft cloth, usually works wonders. It has never damaged any fabric I've used it on, and several mail-order companies sell it.

Professionals You Can Trust

Perhaps most important of all are the old reliables: a good, attentive dry cleaner, a seamstress or tailor, and a good cobbler. Always more expensive than the previous solutions, they are often worth it, especially if you have little faith in your own abilities. Expert help is almost always available for a price. Think of these professionals as your clothes doctors. And, as with physicians, it's best to bring your ailing shoes and garments in to the experts at the earliest sign of distress. Prevention is the best medicine.

Hair

There are so many jokes about bad hair days, epidemiologists should classify them as a plague. The truth is, when your hair looks awful, so do you. But here's the good news: **There is no bad hair, only bad haircuts.** And there are only two simple (but not easy) rules: **Get a great cut** and **keep it clean.**

And here, at last, we're ahead of the Europeans. American hairdressers are flown in to do the models' hair for virtually all of the French and Italian fashion shows. To Continental folk, "American hair" means hair that moves, attracts and reflects the light—hair that is Breck Girl clean, easy and breezy. (Where did they get their info about America from?

Reruns of *Charlie's Angels*?) Well, let's live up to their fantasy.

There is, however, a fantasy that virtually none of us can live up to. If you are trying to model your hairdo after a photo in a magazine or the coiffure of a favorite TV star, be warned. As Chris, my fabulous female hairstylist at Creoza, told me, "First of all, that look you admire has been created for a short-lived camera session by a battalion of specialists who are fooling with lights, cameras, curlers and clips. Unless you have space in your bathroom to bunk a team of pros, forget it!" And that Big Hair that you see on soap stars and female television newscasters is larger than life for a purpose: the TV camera likes exaggeration. What looks right on the small screen is disproportionate in real life. We guarantee that your favorite star's hair looks very different in her private life. So get a good, realistic cut that follows your hair's natural inclination.

The Cut

But, how to get a good hair cut? We all know the horror stories: He promised you the moon but gave you terminal frizzies. It takes some time and experimentation to find a competent, *sympatico*, attentive hairdresser, but it *can* be done. The lack of a good haircut can not only undermine your self-confidence, it can also ruin your credibility. Look at Hillary Clinton! So try to find someone who studies your face, your personality and your life, as well as your hair type, and cuts accordingly. And beware of the gal or guy who gives the same cut to everyone: cookie-cutter hair trends that flatter some clients, but do nothing for others. Also avoid those pushy dictators who manipulate you and make you feel insecure (well, avoid *anyone* who does that!). Amy's hairstylist, Yves Durif, tells her that, sadly, many women subjugate themselves to bad hairdressers because there doesn't seem to be anyone else in their life who ever talks to them or touches them so intimately. I remember one very handsome haircutter I went to who always finished by putting his hands on my shoulders, rubbing seductively and telling me I looked beautiful. (I didn't, and I didn't go back.)

Both Amy and I urge you to judge your hairdresser's work by how it looks right after a cut and simple dry, *not after she/he twiddles and sprays and blows and backcombs it.* Stylish hair is all about a cut appropriate to your hair texture. If stylists have to doctor your locks with curling irons or gels, mousse and other goopy products, they are just covering up *their* shortcomings. *You* won't be able to reproduce that look at home. We aren't the only ones who think this. As Christian Louboutin told us, "I detest a woman who wears solid hair spray." Forget most potions and lotions. They're labor-intensive, expensive and rarely live up to their promises. Remember the point of *Simple Isn't Easy*: Take the time to get it simple and right, then stick to it. You should be able to style your hair at home with just a brush, comb, blow dryer, and—at most—a little dab of product and a few squirts of spray. (If you find yourself staring hopelessly into the mirror each morning yearning for a wig, you are definitely on the wrong track.) Also, remember that hair salons make a lot of profit by selling these highly marked-up products which so often end up collected and unused. If your hairdresser keeps pushing you to buy, find another. And remember the words of Yves the hairdresser. "A good haircut *is* a hairstyle."

Coloring and Perms

Generally, the rule here is respect your hair's natural color and texture, and it will behave kindly to you in return! With few exceptions, drastic departures from what nature endowed you with will never produce the results you desire. Also, they are never simple or easy to accomplish. There are beautiful, looks-enhancing styles for every hair type. In general, it's best not to be in a battle against your kinks, your curls or your ramrod-straight hair. It's a losing fight. Fried, frizzled hair—overbleached and overpermed—rarely looks stylish. Most of us are simply too prone to the "grass is greener" (or curlier, or blonder, or redder) syndrome. Have you ever noticed that the curly-headed want straight hair, the straight-haired want curls, the thick-tressed want fine hair, and the fine-haired want volume? (Okay, we admit that blondes never want to be brunettes, but *they* have to put up with "dumb-blonde" jokes.) Carried to its logical conclusion, we have to deduce that all hair types are desirable to someone. Make peace with yours.

Remember, self-acceptance is the basic condition for style.

As far as covering the grey goes, we know women who do and women who don't. You can look great either way. Liz Tilberis, editor-in-chief of *Harper's Bazaar*, wears her silver-white hair in an adorable pixie cut that looks not only fantastically chic but a whole lot younger than most "cover-the-grey" solutions. But many women feel that grey hair is aging, and it certainly will change the way your makeup and clothes look. If you feel you must color the grey, then be sure to keep up with the roots; nothing looks worse than partly colored hair.

Eyebrows

And while we're on hair, don't forget to groom your eyebrows too. Eyebrows give the face a great deal of its expression and definition. Fabulous faces have distinctive brows: Think of Elizabeth Taylor, Brooke Shields, Audrey Hepburn, Linda Evangelista.

Nails

Short and soft is just right for a pair of ankle socks, but it's hardly what we strive for in our nails. My nails are baby soft and tear like paper. Amy's split, peel and break before they reach the end of her fingertips, and since early adolescence she has tried every remedy, from Knox gelatin drink to glues, wraps, tips and powders. (The drink didn't hurt, but all the other messy fixes were time-consuming, expensive and finally unhealthy.)

Amy found manicurist Elizabeth Lata who, like a skilled gardener, got rid of all the artifice and helped her to cultivate healthier nails. She forced her to wear them short and merely buffed, with no polish. After all those years of wearing scarlet on her fingertips, Amy was surprised to behold her bare hands. But now she loves them. The look is clean, simple and chic, and she can rush out of the salon without that agonizingly long drying session.

I let my nails grow a bit, but Lee at Nails Noble taught me to use a nail strengthener, not just a polish. Sara, the boss, found me a neutral color that she calls "Olivia beige." Now I don't worry about my fingertips clashing with my coat, or my polish chipping. Hallelujah! What a relief!

Good grooming means your nails must be clean, your cuticles and hangnails well-tended. If your nails are naturally strong, and take polish and longer lengths well, fine and wonderful. Otherwise, retract those Dragon Lady claws. (Incidentally, if you look at magazine photos of models, you will seldom see very long nails.) But if varnished talons are part of your trademark style, that's fine. My friend Rose Nappi couldn't do without her lengthy, brightly polished fingernails. One even has her initial on it. To Rose, they're worth the upkeep and time.

Just remember—always keep them neat. Chipped polish is to fingers what runs are to stockings. It's a sure way to mar your carefully cultivated look.

Pedicures may not be quite as visible or important as manicures, but consider: To begin with feet are not usually the fine point of our anatomy. Yet we depend on them for locomotion, and all too often stuff them in shoes that are too tight, too high and too pointy. Then we wonder why our dogs bark. Keep them free of calluses, hangnails, etc., and cut, file, buff or polish those ten little piggies. (By the way, the red Amy used to wear on her fingers now goes on her toes!) If you are thinking, "Well, it's just too much trouble, after all, nobody sees my toes except me," take this advice from Gloria Vanderbilt. When, as a young girl, she asked an older woman why she wore such expensive, lovely underwear when no one saw it, her friend said, "But *I* do!" It's a good mantra to apply universally—to the linings of your jackets, the inside of your purse, and to all that is hidden from everyone but you. *You* are your most important audience.

Skin

F. Scott Fitzgerald wrote, "Let me tell you about the very rich. They are different from you and me." He was right, but only in one important respect: They have better skin.

Nothing compares with the look of clean, clear, well-moisturized, glowing skin. Liz Lee, a model with one of the longest careers in the business, says, "Good skin is something every agency looks for in a girl. She can always lose weight, but she can't fake a good complexion." Almost every celebrity we have seen in person has that one trait in common—flawless skin. The camera loves it. Are they born with it or do they acquire it through good habits? Do constant saunas, steam baths, facials and exercise create that glow? We don't know for sure, but if you weren't lucky enough to be blessed with the genes you deserve, then at least practice the *hygiene* that will bring the best out of yours.

No artist would paint a beautiful picture over a mottled, grease-stained canvas, so why apply makeup over ill-kempt skin? The glow of skin, like the light of a diamond, shines from beneath the surface. Skin cleanliness is not only about keeping the outermost layer dirt-free with good soaps and lotions. It is about deeper cleaning—getting out all the oil, dirt and dead cells embedded in your pores. This is tricky to do on your own, but steaming and masks will help. If it's at all possible to spend the money—you have, after all, saved a bundle on clothing, hair and nail care already!—get regular professional facials. As Simi, Amy's facialist at New York's Stephen Knoll salon, says, "Facials should not be thought of as a luxury, or something to do only on vacation. In Europe even women with modest means habitually put some money aside for their facials."

A good facial isn't about patting and rubbing your face—it's about opening the pores, cleaning out whiteheads and blackheads and then closing pores and toning the skin. It's not always a pleasant process, having someone peer at the side of your nose through a magnifying glass as they press out old dirt, but it is worth it. If the facialist is good, it shouldn't hurt much nor should your face be red as a strawberry when you walk out. And, like your hairdresser, she shouldn't be too pushy with products either. (A very useful tip: Many dermatologists employ a facialist whose services are covered by insurance.)

Meanwhile, don't be fooled and shamed by department store saleswomen who wipe your face with a product and show you the results—a grey cotton ball. No, you are not filthy. We all are constantly shedding the top layer of skin and it looks grey on the cotton. Big deal! That kind of wiping does not do deep cleansing.

Because the point here is to keep it simple, once your skin is clean, it doesn't need much else. Most dermatologists agree that a single moisturizer can do the work of an eye cream, a day cream and a night cream (though Amy insists on all three).

If you have chronic problems with acne or rashes, or have bad pock marks that bother you, we urge you to consult a first-rate dermatologist, or, if necessary, a topflight plastic surgeon to get whatever help you can. (One tip: Avoid plastic surgeons who advertise. The best doctors get their patients from referrals by satisfied clients or other doctors.) With all physicians, a hospital or academic affiliation is one important sign of competence. A good dermatologist will tell you that 90 percent of the promises on commercial skin products are either outright lies or exaggerations. My dermatologist, Dr. Michael Reed, got me over an embarrassing (and late-to-bloom) case of acne that struck me at thirty. No cosmetics helped. What I needed was a few doctor-prescribed medicines. Now, no problems.

Makeup

Now that your skin is looking lovelier, what to put on it? Makeup, like clothing, is an indicator of personality and another means of self-expression. To start, you need to know how you want to look. Once again, this is where some contemplation is necessary. Who are you? What do you really look like and how do you want to appear? As we recommended for your wardrobe, the goal here is to know yourself, simplify your approach and find a makeup routine and stick with it. As Michelle Carr, makeup artist at FACE Stockholm in New York, says, "Natural doesn't mean no makeup—it means proper color to look polished."

Long ago Amy gave up her paintbrushes to write. But every morning she still picks up her makeup brushes and goes to work, creating a self-portrait. The art of applying makeup begins with the tools. Cosmetics are only as good as the implements used to apply them. Start out with a good set of brushes—and then go through your mounds of makeup like a *Simple Isn't Easy* pro. That blue liner that you bought five tubes of five years ago when you were convinced it was the secret to beautiful eyes—into the trash. The twelve colors of blush? Nobody needs more than two. The eyelash curler that you mean to use every morning, but you run out of time? In the garbage. The sparkly green shadow that you used three Halloweens ago, and are saving for the next costume party—waste-basket fodder. Those makeup kits with the seven hundred colors, stubby little tools, and stunted mascara that dried up the week you bought it—none of these hold the key to a pared-down routine. Once you've sorted through your cosmetic chest, examine what's left—the stuff you actually use. (We hope more than a single Q-tip!) Look once more through the dregs and see what else you can toss. Whatever is left could be the basis of your daily makeup ritual.

And forget the old-fashioned idea of "a different look for evening." Your day makeup, with a slight increase in intensity, will suffice. And think of all the time and money and product shelf-space you save.

Some Basic Makeup Tips:

Get a makeup sponge. One tip that almost anyone can benefit from is to use a sponge to apply base. Fingers just don't do the job. Amy uses "wonder wedges" by the dozen. I prefer tiny natural sea sponges. And throw them out often. Dirty sponges are breeding grounds for skin problems.

When you find a product or a look that works, stick with it. As with clothing, if one day your face is pale and lips are carmine, while the next you go for a bottle-based California tan, you don't have a look. We see lots of faces we admire, from the most natural "non-made-up" makeup to the stylized extremes. But a new face each day can be unsettling.

Avoid those "free" makeovers. They are usually nothing more than product-pushing. (They always paint me up like a clown, anyway.) The old expression that when you pay nothing, you get what you pay for applies here. If you *really* are unsatisfied with your current makeup regimen, find a skilled cosmetologist, pay for the session and learn to apply it.

Buy multiples of a favorite product. Since colors are often discontinued, buy what you like in quantity. Store the extra makeup in the refrigerator to ensure freshness and longevity.

Don't swap makeup. Eye infections, herpes, acne and rashes are all contagious. There's no reason for using anyone else's mascara wand or lipstick, ever.

Lip pencils or lip liners. Used under lipstick, these prolong the staying power of your lip color.

Ignore those ubiquitous gift-with-purchase promotions. Unless the product given away is one you actually already use and like—notice that they rarely are—forget about "gifts" and giveaways. Invariably, you wind up buying more stuff than you need to get a useless gift. And it all clutters up your makeup shelf, which should be as streamlined and organized as your closet.

As a general rule, makeup should be used to enhance or exaggerate facial features that you want to draw attention to, rather than to hide what you don't like or create what you don't have. "The best way to look good is to enhance what one already has, simply and easily," says makeup-artist-to-the-stars Kevyn Aucoin. Unless you're going kabuki, don't paint on a second face. Dark slashes will not fool anyone into believing you have cheekbones or deep-set eyelids where there are none. Thin lips will just look a mess if you draw an outline far outside your natural lip line to pretend they are fuller. This makeup-as-camouflage technique sometimes works for photos, but not real life. As Evy, a makeup artist with MAC cosmetics, says, "You want people to look at your eyes, not your eye makeup." Michelle Carr of FACE Stockholm says the most common makeup mistake she sees is that "a lot of women don't trust their eyes. That's where they pile it on too thick and they don't need to."

Amy likes to *slightly* exaggerate her natural pallor with foundation, powder and dark red lipstick, and accentuates her almond-shaped eyes with dark, slanting liner on the upper lid only. I emphasize my large round eyes with contouring shadows, and keep my lips, which already have a lot of natural pigment, relatively pale. Our approaches are very different but they have one thing in common: We both have our makeup routine down pat. If we can't quite get made up with our

183

eyes shut, we at least can get through that A.M. paint-and-powder session with a minimum of thought—and hardly any time. As Diana Vreeland, who could apply her Chinese red lipstick perfectly without even a glance in the mirror, said, "Do you think that after all these years I don't know where these old lips are?"

The style of your makeup should take its cues from the style of your clothes (both based, of course, on the identity you have found for yourself, thanks to *Simple Isn't Easy*). Amy likes a certain amount of exotic artifice, in keeping with her urbane, very styl-ized, high-fashion wardrobe. Her makeup and cloth-ing are almost like a fashion drawing. My cosmetic palette, like that of my wardrobe, is all about low-key neutrals. Is your style sporty, girlish, businesslike, tai-lored, flamboyant? Figure it out, and then be sure your makeup complements your persona.

We don't have to mention that outdoorsy clothes don't go with eyes laden with starry lashes and lips sparkling with magenta frost. A scrubbed, bare face won't do with satin flounces and bows. And *don't* match your makeup colors to your wardrobe. No turquoise eyeliner to match your belt. Your makeup colors should take their cue from your hair and skin coloring, not your poison-green pullover. The shades you choose should be universal enough to go with everything you wear. And what's this thing about lip-stick? Do they multiply in the medicine cabinet? Every woman I know has twenty, though they don't wear most of them. At the most have two or three lipstick shades—one to contrast with your complexion, and another one or two to blend with it.

If you resist all advice about makeup, then do yourself a favor and at least heed these two most basic suggestions:

Blend, blend, blend—no lines of demarcation for blush, powder, foundation, shadows— for the most professional finish.

Amy swears by translucent face powder beneath and on top of her makeup to achieve this polished effect. Of course, all rules are made to be broken and I did see a young girl with Day-Glo orange lips and thin, orange lines painted along her upper lashes. She looked fabulous, but it's not for everyone. And she was under seventeen.

Take 10 to 15 minutes *maximum* putting on your makeup—otherwise something is wrong.

If your routine isn't quick, it's too complicated. Or you're simply wearing too much makeup. Unless, of course, you like that Tammy Faye look, and then you're on your own.

Scents

A woman's scent should be both wonderful and mysterious. And, like any good mystery, it shouldn't be obvious from ten feet away. A perfume should neither announce your arrival, nor leave behind a trail like a diesel's exhaust. It should be semi-private, inhaled only by those whose privilege it is to come close to you. A Frenchman we know fondly recalls how on the first day of school his *maman* tucked her perfume-scented handkerchief into his pocket so that he wouldn't feel too lonely for her. This touching tale could never be told of a woman with multiple perfume personalities.

Scents are powerful and often unconscious manipulators. Whenever I smell library paste I think of my kindergarten classroom and Mrs. Ackerman, my teacher. And they can be invisible turn-offs as well. Once, as a teenager, I had a huge crush on a poetic blond boy who avoided me. Years later, after college, we met again and he confessed he hated the smell of my face—an inoffensive skin cleanser that, unfortunately for me, reminded him of his dad's aftershave!

A scent is linked with your identity, so we suggest you find one and remain faithful. It's more sophisticated and much simpler. Pay no attention to those perfume purveyors who tell you to have a morning scent, an evening scent and a scent for each season. They are already selling the fashion industry's most highly marked-up product.

But once again, don't buy cheap brands, or nasty knock-offs of famous brands. Their scent often changes over time as it reacts with your skin. As my friend Connie insists, "Honest body odor smells a hell of a lot better than stink water." (And don't you think it's odd 'that a certain skin lotion is used as a no-fail bug repellent? What, we ask, does it *attract*?) Finally, don't make the mistake of letting other scented products fight against your signature scent. You weaken and confuse your olfactory image when you layer on scented hair spray, deodorant, skin cream and bath gel. Buy coordinated products, or "scent-free" ones.

Remember, with perfume, simple is not only easier, it is the only way to go.

CHANGING YOUR STYLE

or

What? After All This Work!

"Attachment is the great fabricator of illusions; reality can be attained only by someone who is detached."
—Simone Weil

There comes a time in many women's lives when a change in style is in order. Such a moment may occur after a divorce, a career change, a significant birthday, relocation, major hair recoloring, motherhood or a new marriage. You feel like molting your old, tired skin and showing off a fresh new one. So even though you have now found yourself in your closet and discovered your best personal style, there's still a chance you may one day outgrow it. *This is not to say that any time the circumstances of your life alter you must reinvent yourself.* We think of this future event—if it happens—not as a schizophrenic-like switching of identities but as a healthy, usually subtle evolution from one phase of your life to another.

And—even if your life doesn't take on a new dramatic turn—there are shifts in taste and fashion that inevitably occur over time. No, we hasten to remind you, we are *not* advocating jumping on top of every new trend. We simply mean updating, or editing a bit. So, if you have found a tried-and-true, enduring look for yourself, you probably will find that in order not to look frozen in time, like a prehistoric ant preserved in amber, you will need to make slight, periodic adjustments to update your style. We've all seen many a little lady trundling up the avenue, a victim of what Amy calls "image arrest." Amy remembers in particular seeing an ash blonde with a beehive hairdo, false eyelashes, frosted pink lipstick, in a short, fitted, leopard coat, her look freeze-framed circa 1962. But the year was 1982! And though she was a charmingly eccentric sight, she also inspired pity. These "image arrest" women seem to be communicating through their clothes, hair and makeup that they were last happy two, three or four decades ago.

We reiterate: We do not advise following every trend to try to keep up with fashion. Emanuel Ungaro says, "Many women make the mistake of following trends rather than looking at themselves in the mirror." Bill Blass, the American fashion institution, told us that "committing to trends is the most common wardrobe mistake I see women making." You'll only end up looking like a fad-follower, not a woman of style. Remember Yves Saint Laurent's words, "Fashion changes but style is eternal." If you look at photographs of stylish women over the decades you will notice only in retrospect how they updated their style. They achieved a goal of personal style despite the paradox presented by fashion. They kept changing yet remaining the same. Of course, many had the luxury of being able to afford to wear whatever they wanted, and yet each had picked a fairly consistent look. (So, for that matter, has Cher. Outrageous, but she can both afford and justify the Bob Mackies and Chrome Hearts biker gear, and all that goes with it.) As the designer Valentino, who dressed Jackie for many years, notes, "Almost by magic, Jackie Onassis kept in fashion without significantly altering her look.

Maybe the pant lengths varied a little bit, the hair got longer or shorter, the skirt length changed a few inches. But the look was consistent, constant and fabulous in a outdoorsy American way."

Updating gradually is the ideal way to keep your style, without either scrambling after trends or falling into the sad trap of "image arrest." The paradox is that a classic must change somewhat to remain endlessly attractive to the contemporary eye. It's a company secret that the classic cubic Chanel No. 5 perfume bottle is, every now and then, slightly modified to ensure that its "timeless design" never dates. In the deco period, the flask had sharp, hard edges, but by the Fifties, when industrial design tastes changed, the bottle had gotten more rounded so it didn't seem out of place among the fat curves of automobiles and kidney-shaped coffee tables. Yet, despite its small variations, the bottle has never lost its identity, and nobody even noticed it changed. This principle, if we could apply it to ourselves, would be the perfect approach. As writer Annette Tapert, author of *The Power of Style,* says, "You don't invent yourself once and for all. Style is an ongoing creative process."

But unfortunately, none of us has a team of industrial designers to tweak our style when necessary. How did they know *when* to update the Chanel bottle? How do *you* know when your look has grown stale? Here's a handy questionnaire that may help.

If you mark one "yes," consider a change. If you've checked "yes" two or more times, definitely give it a shot. Consult this list again a year from now, or every so often.

Have you made a major physical change lately (lost a lot of weight, changed hair style or color, etc.)? Y N

Do you need to put together a post-diet, slimmer wardrobe? Y N

Are you readjusting after moving to another climate? Y N

Do you need to create a wardrobe for pregnancy or motherhood? Y N

Do you need to change your wardrobe to suit a new job? Y N

Does the need for change strike you with the force of a revelation? Y N

Is there is a consensual tide that you can no longer stem? Y N

PUTTING TOGETHER A WARDROBE
AFTER A PHYSICAL CHANGE

Needless to say, if you lose a lot of weight, gain it or change your looks in any other major way (cosmetic surgery, major hair style renovation, etc.), your wardrobe will (or should) be affected. When an older friend of ours simply decided to stop dyeing her hair and let it grow in a fabulous silver, she found that very few of her clothes looked the same. She'd gone from a dramatic brunette to an equally dramatic but very pale look. Her clothes had to change. If you go blonde, if you tan, even if you make a dramatic change in your makeup, hairstyle or contact lens color, you may have to rethink at least some of your wardrobe and that may mean shopping. *But not before you go back to chapter 3 and start over.*

READJUSTING AFTER MOVING TO ANOTHER CLIMATE

After years up north, I moved to Florida and found that I didn't have the right clothes. It wasn't just that I needed to trade my wool pants for linen ones. I discovered that the sunlight, the lifestyle and the expectations were different in Florida. People dressed more casually than I did in the daytime, but got more dressy than I was used to at night. Weird. It took me a while to figure out what would work, especially given the complication that I always needed a sweater or jacket to cope with air conditioning. If *you* relocate, you may find that you need to rethink your wardrobe completely. But don't rush into it. Make do with one or two new outfits from your preexisting spring and summer wardrobes until you figure out what will work. By day I still dress more formally than a lot of Floridians, and I'm still not in sequins at night, but my wardrobe *is* different. And I'm comfortable with it.

CREATING A WARDROBE FOR YOUR PREGNANCY OR MOTHERHOOD

Amy says pregnancy is difficult enough without adding the burden of not knowing what to wear! Those castoffs that friends lend you and those potato sacks that mothers-in-law buy are guaranteed to be more nauseating than morning sickness. Nancy Robinson, who worked on this manuscript, told us, "I was given a maternity dress by my sister and it was enormous! I already felt pretty immense, but when I put that dress on, I felt like I needed a 'Wide Load' sign across my behind." Lots of women try to get through their pregnancies without shopping at all—since there are already so many extra expenses. But they often end up depressed and depressing-looking—not to mention uncomfortable—in stretched-out knits and old floppy shirts. Instead, using our *Simple Isn't Easy* philosophy, remember that one or two good-looking dresses are better than a pile of ugly borrowed or cheaply bought goods.

On the other hand, pregnancy can be a time to also incubate a permanent new style. Miriam discarded her stagnating vampy look—high heels, heavy liner, red lips—during her first pregnancy and continued her new look once she became a full-time mother. A practical soul, she never looked back. "I feel much more myself now in flats and no eye makeup—it just started to feel too heavy on me," she says. With her very dark, well-defined features and her ballerina's grace, she will never look dowdy in this new, simplified, stylish—but more motherly—guise.

195

Other changes may take place. To her horror, Amy's feet grew a size after pregnancy, and she has been gradually rebuilding her shoe wardrobe ever since. (At last! A legitimate excuse to buy shoes!) Finally, realize that you may already have suitable maternity wear in your closet. Amy found that most of her clothing with no defined waist (i.e. trapeze dresses, big jackets) saw her through her entire pregnancy. The only real maternity wear she bought were skirts. And don't listen to comments about how the hemline on a nonmaternity dress will rise higher in the front than the back. Who cares? It looks cute. You *are* pregnant, after all.

CHANGING YOUR WARDROBE TO SUIT A NEW JOB

Diana Vreeland's life, says a former colleague, could be neatly divided into "the turban phase, the snood phase, and the Alexandre haircut period." She wore the turban when she was a young married lady of leisure. She adopted the snood when she began working as fashion editor for *Harper's Bazaar*. When she took over as editor-in-chief of *Vogue*, she lost the headgear and wore a sleek hairdo, invented by the great French hairdresser Alexandre. She kept that hairdo—which Andre Leon Talley calls "the black Kabuki flip"—for the rest of her days. The lesson to benefit from here is: *Be never quite in style, and never quite out of style.* And always have a style that makes sense for your job.

WHEN THE NEED FOR CHANGE STRIKES YOU
WITH THE FORCE OF A REVELATION

A fashion editor friend of Amy's says that sometimes she puts on an outfit that looked exactly right a season or two ago, and suddenly, one day it seems all wrong—shoulders too big, length too long, silhouette too baggy. "It's like discovering a stranger where there once was a friend," she says. Maybe you've experienced that odd awakening. This probably means that, without your even quite knowing it, your eye has readjusted to changes in fashion or your self-image, while your wardrobe hasn't yet caught up. Amy's fashion editor friend compares that sudden revelation with the experience we've all had of, in a flash, realizing it's time for a haircut. "The day before your hair seemed just fine," she says. "And overnight, everything seems to be falling in the wrong place. There's a gap between what exists in your mind's eye, and what you see in the mirror."

My friend Cynthia Kling, marketing representative at *Newsweek*, has a clever approach to updates. "I have a uniform, but each season I try one new thing. Last year it was a pair of spikey, high-heeled pumps. It's not a big investment, but it gives you a chance to update and experiment with your basic look."

So, can we, after all this, be telling you to throw stuff out the minute it "goes out of style"? Nonsense! Take that no-longer-loveable outfit and try retiring it for a while. I know an advertising account executive who buys only high-style designer suits but does tire of them. Still, she never throws them away. "I put them in the hall closet for a vacation," she says. "Then, sometimes after a year or two, sometimes longer, they look fresh again." And if they don't—off to the thrift shop, tag sale, museum, etc.

WHEN THERE IS A CONSENSUAL TIDE THAT YOU CAN NO LONGER STEM

Amy had a friend, Andrea, who was a borderline image-arrest case. Andrea looked quite young, but one makeup habit of hers fixed her age as surely as a number around her neck. She wore dark lip liner which outlined a much paler shade of lipstick. Amy searched her soul every time she saw Andrea, thinking of a delicate way to advise her to match lip liner to lipstick shade, but the words failed her. She even talked to me about it, but I advised her to keep her mouth shut! (A girlfriend once told me my hair color looked "cheap" and I've never forgiven her!) Then to Amy's surprise and relief, one day Andrea showed up in class with a single, uniform color upon her lips. "I've had so many people tell me to drop the dark lip liner," Andrea explained to Amy without her even having to ask. "I just never thought I could get used to seeing myself any other way. But I'm so glad I listened—I now see how much better I look."

If you hear over and over the same chorus of advice from disparate, well-intentioned friends (or well-meaning strangers), you *might* want to consider trying out that recommendation, to cut or color your hair, shorten your skirt, add eyebrow pencil—whatever. Amy has had the courage, by the way, to point out gently to a few extremely close friends, including her sister, that it might in fact be time to pluck their eyebrows, or grow them out, or reevaluate the use of a curling iron. She changed her entire makeup routine herself after a pre-party cosmetic session with a trustworthy friend, and every now and then she asks that same friend if another change is due.

"Fashion changes, but style is eternal."
—*Yves Saint Laurent*

IN CLOSING

And that, dear reader, is that. You have all the information and motivation you could possibly need to create and keep an effective and stylish wardrobe going. I think you would have to agree that while our solutions, suggestions and recommendations have been simple, they have not been easy. But at this point you should be launched on a new, more comfortable and more organized way of dressing. And hey, isn't that *you* in the mirror looking stylish, with a style that's all your own!

Letter to Readers

Did *Simple Isn't Easy* help you? We're interested in knowing how you applied our ideas to your own life. Do you have any tricks of your own that women might benefit from? We would like to incorporate some reader responses into a new edition of *Simple Isn't Easy*. Please send your comments, suggestions and questions to us, care of our publisher: Harper-Paperbacks, Dept SE, 10 East 53rd Street, New York, NY 10022.

Sincerely and stylishly,

Olivia & Amy

P.S.

Send us before and after pictures, of yourself *and* your closet!